MURDER AT THE CONVENT

Book One
Joe McCullen Cozy Mystery Series

Tanya R. Taylor

BOOK TWO IN THIS EXCITING, NEW COZY MYSTERY SERIES!

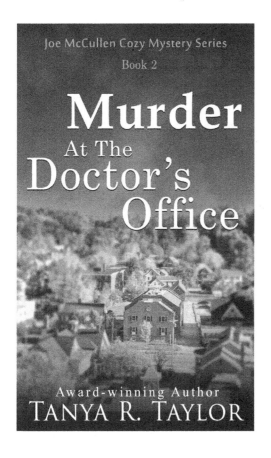

Joe McCullen Cozy Mystery Series
Book 2

Murder
At The
Doctor's
Office

Award-winning Author
TANYA R. TAYLOR

NOTE TO THE READER

In this book, the nuns have been given regular surnames so as not to confuse the storyline.

I hope that you enjoy the read!

Saturday morning, an ear-piercing scream could be heard throughout the grounds of the convent in South Pickstock. Eleven nuns all ran in the direction of the shrilling scream only to find Sister Anna Gunter kneeling at the side of Mother Elizabeth Rhinehart's lifeless body on the floor of her room.

There was a collective gasp.

"Mother!" Angelica Gottlieb hurried over to the horrendous scene before them. "What happened?" she demanded of the twenty-three-year-old postulant who'd only been a member of the convent for approximately two months.

Anna's face was drenched with tears. "I don't know! I met her here like this," she replied, frantically.

Then Angelica's eyes widened as she noticed the bloody knife in Anna's hand.

"I…I…just picked it up!" Anna exclaimed as she sensed what the nun was thinking. "Someone did this to her."

Gertrude, a tall, heavyset, no-nonsense woman went over to the nightstand and emptied out the contents of a small grocery bag. She then approached Anna and holding the bag said, "Put it in here." Gertrude was as cool as a cucumber.

Anna quickly dropped the knife into the bag.

"We must call the police now!" Angelica said.

"No police just yet," Gertrude replied. "We must notify the archbishop first."

She left the room and, in the hallway, picked up the handset from the wall. Rosa Perez, a nun in her late forties, around the same age as Gertrude, and who'd entered the convent around the same time as she had, looked on at Gertrude as she made the call, her eyes darting back occasionally at their fallen mother.

The conversation was brief and Gertrude's demeanor had not altered.

"The archbishop is on his way," Gertrude stated upon reentering the room. "His secretary will be calling the police."

Anna was now standing in another nun's embrace. They all, except for Gertrude, were weeping and looking somberly at the shocking sight at their feet.

"Who could've done this?" Angelica exclaimed.

"This can't be possible!" Sarah Robinson, the eldest nun who'd finally made her way there by means of her walking cane cried. "This is a convent, for goodness' sake!"

Claire Hans, a sixty-year-old who'd just celebrated her thirtieth year in the consecrated life, hurried over to her to offer a helping hand. "Someone must've broken in," she said.

"And if that's true, it's possible that they're still here," Angelica noted, approaching the door.

"Where are you going?" Gertrude asked.

"I'm going to take a look around. Perhaps, the rest of us are in danger too."

"Well, you're not going alone. I'm coming with you." She looked back at her sisters. "Lock this door behind us."

Claire hurried over to do just that.

The women walked out into the hallway together, sticking within inches of each other. They both felt a knot in their throats as they cautiously proceeded. The convent was large with long hallways and the walls echoed with each step. The sisters were unarmed, felt like easy prey, and hoped that at the end of their unwanted tour, they would arrive back to their former location safely.

"Slow down!" Angelica told Gertrude.

Gertrude looked at her. "How much slower do you want me to go? If we go any slower, it may take hours to check this place."

They made their way to the kitchen and Gertrude looked around as Angelica checked the back door.

Twisting the knob, she said, "It's locked—from the inside, of course. And the latch is still in place."

As they came upon the sitting and dining rooms, one of them went inside while the other kept watch in the hallway in case there was any movement. The end of the hallway led into another which curved right and on both sides were the individual cells.

"I'll check my own room," Gertrude said, gruffly.

"Be my guest," Angelica answered, as Gertrude went in.

Angelica barely blinked while keeping an eye on the hallway, hoping that no one would spring out in front of her from one of the rooms.

"Hurry up!" She whispered loudly in Gertrude's direction.

"All clear." Gertrude returned.

They continued along and a few doors down, Gertrude gave her the nod to go and check her room.

Angelica went inside and within moments, she was out of there.

"Let's keep going," she said.

"You checked that quickly?"

"How big do you think my room is?"

Gertrude rolled her eyes. Sighing, she replied, "We need to check the bookstore."

"The bookstore?" Angelica grimaced.

"Yes—the bookstore."

"But…"

"But what, Sister?"

"The bookstore is quite spacious and I'm afraid to go in there without the police being present."

Gertrude thought for a second. "Okay, I'll go in and make a quick inspection. You wait here."

"I don't think that's a wise idea," Angelica told her. "I wouldn't want you to risk being harmed."

Gertrude sighed again. "We came this far and the bookstore is right through that door just ahead. It only makes sense that we check there too. If it's clear, then we know the killer has left. Got it?"

Reluctantly, Angelica nodded. "Okay."

Gertrude continued toward the blue door which was the side entrance to the bookstore. She never appreciated that the store was adjacent to the main building where their rooms were located. However, everyone else agreed the deadlock on the inside provided adequate security for them. As she approached, she could clearly see that the door was still locked.

"I guess this is a waste of time," she muttered as she opened the door and stepped inside the store.

Angelica was looking on nervously and making the sign of the cross.

The bookstore was closed for business every Saturday so that the nuns could unite for a midday meeting, do extra charitable work, and accomplish other duties before evening Mass.

Having a bookstore on the convent grounds had been Mother Elizabeth's dream. She insisted that literature played an important role in spreading the Gospel and she wanted people to feel comfortable coming there and exploring the many books available to the public. Gertrude loved reading as well. Her mother used to be a librarian and had always brought home books for her brother and her to read which were quite often their only form of entertainment. The family could not afford a TV until Gertrude was already in her late teens. After school and on weekends, she spent hours engrossed within the pages of a novel and often felt at the end of the good ones like the characters and entire atmosphere by which she'd been enlightened were real.

Whenever she went into the convent's bookstore, she felt like she'd entered a new world of possibilities, with hope and faith for fellow parishioners and for those seeking deeper spiritual fulfilment.

The area was approximately eighteen hundred square feet with rows of shelves each situated five feet apart. The walls had been painted a light peach hue that Mother Elizabeth felt gave the place a lighthearted sort of vibe. Gertrude tended to agree. At the front, near the entrance, was the cashier's desk and a few feet away from it was a small showcase where various medals were displayed, some attached to stainless steel necklaces encased in plastic wrapping. At the rear of the bookstore, close to where Gertrude had entered the room, was a glass cabinet stocked with both metal and wooden crosses. The nun in charge of the bookstore—Martha Wingate—found that the cabinet at the back needed regular restocking as people often came in looking for crosses to hang in their homes or offices. Some claimed their house or apartment was haunted and needed them for protection. Martha had heard many of the strangest stories in her day, but never doubted that those sharing their experiences with her wholeheartedly believed in what they were saying.

Gertrude started through the aisle nearest to the access door, then as she made it nearly halfway through, she asked, "Is there anyone in here?" She wasn't expecting or hoping for a response as the very thought of receiving one made her cringe. She figured some nuns wouldn't know how to defend themselves if the situation were to arise, but she knew she wouldn't hesitate to use the martial arts training she'd received many years ago in her late teens. She was not one to fold up in fear and take whatever came her way. She had the philosophy that as a nun she could be pious, but tough whenever she needed to be.

Just as she'd expected, no one answered her. And when she made it to the front of the store, she quickly checked the front door which happened to be locked. She then slowly crossed each aisle, looking to her right to see if there was, perhaps, someone hiding out. After she took a turn through the last aisle on the southern end of the store and realized the coast was clear, she breathed a sigh of relief.

Reentering the hallway of the convent, she locked the door behind her. Angelica was still standing there looking as if she'd held her breath the entire time she was gone.

"No one's in there," Gertrude said, approaching her.

Angelica smiled, resting her hands on her chest. "Thank heavens!"

"Let's go back to the others," Gertrude said.

As they headed back to Mother Elizabeth's room, Gertrude looked at Angelica. "Do you realize that each of the doors were locked?" she asked.

"Yes, I do," Angelica replied, feeling rather uneasy with the direction in which she feared the conversation might be going.

"I would hate to think…"

"Don't say it, Sister Gertrude! Just don't say it because it can't be so."

"If you don't hear it from me, Sister, we'd all likely be hearing it from the police anyway. So, you'd might as well face the reality of what might have happened here," Gertrude replied, matter-of-factly.

"You can't possibly think that Anna…"

"How well do we know her?" she interjected. "We all know how hard Mother Elizabeth can be on us for the slightest things and Anna was no exception to her short temper. I imagine it was tough on her during her transition here and she probably even wondered if this was truly her calling."

"Mother was seventy-three years old. I think she had a right to be a bit crotchety sometimes," Angelica replied in Mother Elizabeth's defense.

"A bit?" Gertrude grimaced.

"Well—a lot, to be completely honest. Besides, she had an array of health issues to contend with which could not have made wearing a smile most of the day any easier."

"We all understood Mother and loved her nonetheless with all her flaws just as she loved us, but Anna is such a young, naïve girl who knows nothing about the world and who hasn't yet developed the virtues of wisdom, patience and longsuffering. Perhaps, Mother said something to her which caused her to lose her temper and do the unthinkable."

Angelica stopped in the middle of the hallway. Several more steps and they would be at Mother Elizabeth's door. "How could you possibly suggest that someone who decides to honor God with her life could have it in her to commit such a terrible deed and right inside this convent?" She'd lowered her voice. "In spite of how things look, Gertrude, let's give Anna the benefit of the doubt. There's nothing more terrible than being accused of something you had absolutely nothing to do with. You, of all people, should know better than that!"

Gertrude's countenance fell at the mention of the false accusation once made against her. She had put it in the back of her mind and sealed it off so as not to be plagued by unpleasant memories. However, Angelica had brutally brought it to the surface again.

"I see your point, Sister, but also see mine…" she replied. "If Mother Elizabeth's killer isn't Anna Gunter, then it must be one of us. I suggest you always have eyes in the back of your head because no stranger came through any of these doors or windows."

She marched ahead of her and knocked at the door while Angelica remained paralyzed for a few moments in the hallway by the gravity of her words.

_____

2

Seventeen-year-old Mike Tenney walked inside the rectory that Saturday morning. His aqua blue cotton T-shirt and faded jeans were stained with red dirt from the garden out back.

Father Joe McCullen was sitting in his recliner sipping a tall glass of raspberry punch that Sue McCloud, the church's secretary, had made for him. Sue was more than a secretary; she was Mike Tenney's godmother and had raised the boy ever since his mother, Elisa, who happened to be her best friend, died when Mike was just two years old. His father was out of the picture from the moment Elisa told him that she was pregnant with his child. So, Sue did it all alone, adopted the boy and never married. Mike grew up to be a tall, dark, handsome young man and the star player on his school's softball team.

"Man! That sun's already piping out there!" he exclaimed. "Felt like I was about to be cooked."

"Go and wash up, then sit down and have a midmorning snack," Joe said.

Clean-shaven and proudly bald, Father Joe McCullen was a six-foot-six, giant of a man with a protruding stomach. He was busier than most priests in his diocese, well liked and constantly serving the needs of his community— even those who did not share his faith. He also had a blunt sense of humor that usually made people gravitate towards him.

Mike Tenney returned to the living room a few minutes later in a change of clothing and he was rubbing his hands together.

"Are you suddenly cold or just that hungry?" Joe asked, lowering his eyeglasses slightly.

Mike grinned. "Famished is more like it."

The church's rectory was situated in the northern district of Old Providence, ten miles from South Pickstock, and had been home to the fifty-two-year-old priest for the past fifteen years. He'd been transferred there from another parish.

The little place had undergone major renovations five years earlier. Tarnished, off-white, medium-sized floor tiles had been replaced by large, beige porcelain ones throughout the front area. And new wooden panels replaced the old ones in both bedrooms. Outdated furniture had been substituted for newer, modern designs, including a neat little chandelier which dangled right above the dining room table, where Mike went and sat down after he'd scooped up a big bowl of leftovers.

"Smells like pasta," Joe said, as he switched the channel to the news.

"Yep."

"That's your midmorning snack?"

"Uh-huh." Mike wasted no time diving in.

Joe glanced his way. "When is school starting again?"

"On the fourth of next month."

"All set?"

"Just about."

"You've got two weeks to get everything you need. Your tuition's been paid already, so at least you and your mother don't have to be bothered with that."

"Thanks, Father."

Joe McCullen had been like a substitute father for Mike. There were times when Sue had nowhere to turn when Mike desperately needed the basic necessities and Father Joe offered his assistance. She had known the priest well enough to entrust Mike into his care as a preteen so that he could help around the rectory and Mike, in turn, could acquire a sense of responsibility. She felt Father Joe was the perfect example of a good man and she wanted Mike to emulate him.

At first, Joe was reluctant to have Mike around at such a young age because he said he "didn't like no mix up" and insisted that Sue remained on the premises whenever the boy would be there. Joe had a stellar reputation and intended to keep it that way.

Mike gulped down some water, then continued to tackle his meal. Joe looked at him and shook his head.

"What's the matter, Father?" Mike asked.

"You act as if the food's about to run away. I'm surprised you're not as plump as I am."

Mike grinned. "Hey…where's that pecan pie Mrs. Higginbotham brought by the other day? I didn't see it in the kitchen."

"You mean the pie you said looked absolutely delicious and you didn't bother to take a slice before you went home that day?"

"Yeah—that one."

"Well, it's not here."

"Where is it?" Mike looked at him suspiciously.

"If it's not here, it must mean that it's now someplace else."

"You ate it all. Didn't you?"

"Not the entire thing. I offered a slice to Father Donald at lunch yesterday which he graciously accepted."

The boy sighed.

"What's the matter?" Joe tilted his eyeglasses again. "You and your mom both had an opportunity to take as much of the pie as you wanted, but you took a chance leaving such a delectable pastry with me whom you know have a terribly selfish sweet tooth. Take my money and my car, but don't mess with my pie!"

Mike laughed, shaking his head this time.

"Guess it serves me right getting shared out. I shouldn't have let Mom rush me home to study that evening."

"Don't blame her! You had ample time to get what you wanted before she ever showed up."

Just then, the phone rang and Mike stood up to get up.

"No, sit down and finish your meal." Joe said. "I'll get it."

He went over to the antique table and answered the phone.

"What did you say?" Mike heard Joe say, moments later.

"Mother Elizabeth? It can't be so."

Joe soon ended the call and Mike noticed a confused and horrified expression on his face.

"What's the matter, Father?" he asked.

Joe slowly made it over to the couch and sat down. "Mother Elizabeth's dead. I was told she'd been murdered."

"What?" Mike dropped his fork and went over to the living room with the priest.

"Someone...killed Mother Elizabeth?"

Joe nodded. "Yep—apparently."

"Where? Where did this happen?"

"At the convent."

The front door of the rectory flew open and Sue McCloud rushed inside.

"Father…I heard that Mother Elizabeth's…"

"Yeah. I just got a call from the archbishop's secretary," Joe interjected.

"So, it's true then?" She glanced at Mike, then looked at Joe again.

"I'm afraid so." He got up. "I'd better go and get ready. They'll be here soon. I just had to sit for a few minutes first to digest the news."

"Where are you going?" She asked him.

"The archbishop's driver is coming to pick me up. I'm accompanying His Excellency to the convent."

"Do they know who did it? Who killed her?" Mike asked.

"I don't have any of those details yet," Joe replied, somberly.

As he headed to his bedroom, Sue sat down next to Mike.

"Can you believe it?" she said, worriedly.

"It seems surreal," Mike replied. "I've never heard of anything like this happening before at a convent."

"I'm afraid the devil doesn't have much regard for anything sacred." She sighed. "I hope that whoever the monster is that committed this heinous act will be caught and prosecuted to the fullest extent of the law! Why would anyone possibly want to murder Mother Elizabeth?"

Mike cleared his throat. "Well...to be honest, I can think of at least a dozen reasons why. Everyone hates her."

Sue looked at him as if he'd uttered a forbidden word.

"You forgot how she tried to turn Father Joe against me just last week because she claimed I didn't clip the shrubs on the convent grounds the way they're supposed to be clipped? Accused me of being a lazy bum. That's after I mowed the lawn and raked up all the leaves. She said I was using Father's kindness and just wanted handouts."

Sue sighed again. "You know there was nothing she could've possibly said to turn Father against you. We all know how Mother Elizabeth was. The older she got, the grumpier she became and we all—well…most of us…just excused her behavior."

"Seems like this time she crossed the wrong one," Mike replied.

Just then, they heard a car pull up and Sue quickly stood to her feet. "That must be them!"

She hurried over to the front window, then called for Joe who was just reentering the living room. He was wearing a black coat suit along with his clerical collar.

"I'll be on my way," he said to them. "Remember to secure the place on your way out."

"God bless you, Father." Sue interlaced her fingers and squeezed them tightly. "And God bless the dead."

She made the sign of the cross.

Joe hurried outside to the waiting Lincoln and quickly hopped in the back seat where Archbishop Ronald Simms greeted him.

"Thanks for coming," Simms said as the driver pulled off.

"I was so stunned when I heard the news, sir. I…I'm still stunned. Who on earth could have broken into the convent and committed such an atrocity?" Joe replied.

"It's the devil's work, son. In all my years as a priest, I've never heard of anything like this. Mother Elizabeth was a wonderful person who dedicated her life—the past sixty years to be exact—to the work of The Lord. Living piously and unselfishly with the sisters."

Joe nodded his head, but inside was rolling his eyes. He knew Mother Elizabeth was a *piece of work*, as he sometimes called her behind closed doors, and he doubted she'd be nominated for sainthood. Simms' description of her reminded him of the phony renditions occasionally made at funerals where suddenly, the deceased used to be a kind, loving, wonderful person when, in fact, the opposite was often true.

"Yes, she gave of herself and has impacted the lives of many," Joe said. "And despite her sometimes rambunctious behavior, I don't believe she ever meant any harm."

Archbishop Simms turned slightly in his direction. "Do you think it was someone she knew?"

Joe shrugged. "Anything is possible, sir. I won't sit here and pretend as if everybody loved her. Mother Elizabeth has said and done some hurtful things to some people out there and although we'd never for a moment dream that their anger towards her would persuade them to do the unthinkable, I think we both know that's a possibility."

Simms reassumed his previous position.

Father McCullen was known for his brutal honesty intermingled with a levelheadedness that was admired by many. He was not the type of priest that anyone expected to sugarcoat anything.

"Between you and me, I can't tell you the number of complaints that flooded my office regarding Mother Elizabeth over the past few years," Simms said, much to Joe's surprise.

"Really?"

Simms nodded.

"It was always *something* and quite frankly, apart from speaking with her, which I did on a number of occasions, I didn't know what else to do. She was already up in age. I realized it was probably best that she retired and left the work of the convent to the younger sisters, but she refused to even consider it. She told me once that if I forced her to retire, God would punish me for preventing her from doing her life's work. Naturally, I couldn't find it within myself to retire her anyway. The fact was that she was still doing a lot of good, making a positive impact in the lives of our parishioners by helping out with the Beginners program, the women's charity work and other missions that greatly benefited the work of the church. But for those around her, she was obviously a handful."

"Are you saying that it was the other nuns that made the complaints to your office?" Joe sought clarification.

"Yes," Simms replied. "Some of them submitted written complaints and others called and complained to my secretary, Mrs. Armstrong."

Joe shook his head. "Well, even though anything in this world is possible, I personally doubt that any of the nuns are responsible for what happened to her, despite her being a pain in the butt."

Simms gave him a reprimanding look.

"I'm sorry, sir. That was a slip," Joe quickly did damage control.

"I tend to agree that it would be absurd to think that any of the nuns was involved in her death. So, the killer must've somehow broken into the convent. Perhaps, he was after money that Mother most certainly would've refused to give him."

Joe grinned slightly. "That's one thing he never would've gotten from her even if her life depended upon it!"

As they pulled up to the convent, they met at least a dozen police cars parked haphazardly on the grounds and yellow tape surrounded the edifice. Red and blue lights were still flashing on the roof of some vehicles and officers could be seen inspecting and controlling the scene. Neighbors and passersby stood along the sidewalk across the street, many with the look of dread on their faces. Joe noticed a few women who were in tears, quite possibly at the very thought that a murder could have been committed at such a place.

"Only God knows what we're going to find in there," Simms muttered. "Nevertheless, it's time to go."

The driver quickly got out and opened the door for the archbishop. Joe was getting out at the same time. The scene before him saddened him as the reality of the matter sank in even more deeply within that moment. Suddenly, a flood of memories resurfaced of the days when Mother Elizabeth had done something to make a child smile or gave a beggar a meal, not without first offering him an inspirational word. Before then, Joe barely remembered her smile which seemed absent for the most part, primarily over the past decade. Something inside her had changed and he never could figure out what it was. He did recall saying to himself once that if old age made everyone as miserable as she was, he'd rather die just before hitting seventy. The thought of becoming the sort of person many others reviled *and for good reason too* concerned him.

He and Simms made their way over to the front entrance of the convent and were immediately stopped by the rookie policeman stationed at the door.

"Let them in…" Detective Wally Profado told him after he'd spotted them from the hallway.

The young officer stepped aside and Simms and Joe continued on.

"Thank you, officer," Simms said.

Joe thanked him as well.

"Archbishop…" Wally shook Simms' hand.

"Father Joe…" He turned to him next with a wider smile.

"Thank you for allowing us in, Detective," Joe told him. "As you might imagine, the news regarding Mother's death is very disturbing."

Wally Profado and his wife Elena were faithful members of Father Joe's parish for the past fifteen years and had met with Joe for counselling during a rough patch in their marriage six years earlier. Elena wanted a child more than anything else in the world, but was having a hard time conceiving. Wally couldn't manage to get her to snap out of her depression or to seek counselling. It was only after she'd come across text messages from another woman, clearly interested in her husband, that she was finally interested in seeking counselling. Joe was instrumental in the mending of their relationship and after much prayer and even considering adoption as an alternative, the couple finally had a child of their own two years later.

"This tragedy is shocking to us all, really," Wally responded to Joe's remarks. "But I can tell you we'll solve this." He glanced at the archbishop.

Simms' eyes were focused just ahead toward Mother Elizabeth's room where most of the commotion was going on. Soon, he and Joe watched as a black body bag containing the lifeless body of Mother Elizabeth was wheeled out on a stretcher.

"My God!" Simms' exclaimed. He turned to the detective. "Do you mind…"

"Not at all. Please do," Wally quickly interjected.

Simms approached as the coroners headed in his direction.

"I'd like to say a brief prayer for the deceased," he told the men, who did not object.

Joe watched as Simms prayed over the body, then sealed it with the sign of the cross.

"May her soul rest in peace," he uttered just before the men proceeded to transport the stretcher outside.

Joe and Wally joined the archbishop who, by then, visibly had tears in his eyes.

"This makes no sense," Simms muttered as he retrieved his white handkerchief from his coat pocket.

"I'm afraid it doesn't," Wally replied.

"Do you have any information about what might have happened?" Joe asked Wally.

"We're in the process of speaking with the nuns to find out more. They're being questioned in the eastern wing for now by a couple of my colleagues," Wally said.

"Are we permitted to join them?" Simms asked.

Wally thought for a moment. Then he glanced at Father Joe who had that look in his eyes that Wally was familiar with. It usually meant *I'm counting on you*.

"Okay, this is not the usual practice, Your Excellency, but I'll allow you and Father Joe to be there as moral support for the nuns.

That's really the only way I can sell it to the Chief if he pulls me into his office with a line of questioning surrounding that."

"You're a gem, Wally," Joe said. "We're most grateful."

"Thank you, Detective," Simms added.

oe and Simms accompanied Wally Profado to the conference room inside the east wing of the convent. The nuns were all seated at the large table, along with junior Detectives Sam Jackson and Wendy Kenna who sat together on the southern side.

The chatter stopped the moment the men entered the room, and Joe immediately noticed the look of relief on the faces of the terrified nuns. Gertrude, however, seemed like her old self and even had a rather lighthearted expression on her face.

The nuns stood as the archbishop walked in and the detectives followed suit.

"Good afternoon, everyone," he said. "Sisters—we heard the news and Father Joe and I are here for moral support. Please sit down and assist the good detectives in any way you can as we must get to the bottom of this most horrendous tragedy."

Joe whispered something to the archbishop as the detectives resumed their interrogation of the nuns. He then walked over to a large closet and retrieved two chairs out of it and placed them against a wall a few feet away from where everyone else was seated. Wally, in the meantime, had made his way over to an empty chair at the table.

"You were saying, Sister Angelica..." Detective Kenna stated.

Angelica glanced over at the archbishop and Father Joe. She was so relieved that they were there and now felt more comfortable answering the detectives' questions.

"Yes, I was saying that Mother Elizabeth seemed fine before she retired for the night. I hadn't noticed anything different about her. She hadn't joined us for early morning prayer, but that was not unusual since occasionally, she'd sleep later in the mornings due to the medication she'd taken for her illnesses. The rest of us sisters just go on about our routine."

Kenna nodded. "I understand that now all of you agree that there was nothing strange about Mother Elizabeth's behavior yesterday that might indicate that she was fearful of anything or might've had something weighing heavily on her mind. So, it brings us to question the type of relationship that each of you had with her. As you know, we are still investigating the scene which means that we don't have a lot of answers just yet. And as Sister Gertrude here indicated after having conducted a walk-through along with Sister Angelica, nothing appeared out of place and all the doors were locked from the inside. Isn't that correct, ladies?" She looked at Angelica and Gertrude.

Angelica nodded and Gertrude boldly replied: "Yes, that's correct. Nothing was out of place and all the doors were still locked from the inside."

"I see you have all single hung windows here at the convent that only go up so far."

"Yes!" Gertrude responded.

"So, unless a person's approximately six or seven inches wide, it's almost impossible for an adult to fit through any of the windows. A child can, of course."

"Certainly, but there are no children here, and I doubt a child would've slain Mother Elizabeth," Gertrude said, matter-of-factly.

"This is very strange," Detective Jackson chimed in. "So, I'm sure you understand that we must cover all bases to get to the bottom of this case."

Some heads were nodding, including Joe's.

"So, let's start with you, Sister Anna— since you were the one to find Mother Elizabeth deceased in her room," Kenna said.

Anna Gunter's face was drenched with tears as she'd been sobbing the entire time since discovering the body of their mother superior. Angelica was sitting next to her as a means of support as it was clear to her that the young lady was falling apart. She'd been the first one to welcome Anna into their community and taught her many things, including what she thought was the best way for the postulant to interact with Mother Elizabeth in order to keep the peace and to stay within God's will.

"What type of relationship did you have with Mother Elizabeth?" Kenna asked Anna.

Anna looked Angelica's way who immediately nodded and offered a slight smile.

She took a breath in and sought to compose herself. "Well, I guess you can say that

I got into trouble quite a lot with Mother Superior."

"What kind of *trouble*?" Kenna asked.

"I was responsible for the laundry, along with Sisters Rachel and Abigail. Usually, I was reprimanded by Mother for not folding the clothes properly. I thought I was doing it right, but she wanted them done a special way, particularly the blouses, and I sometimes forgot to fold the sleeves in half before tucking them under the back of the blouse. It was very confusing to me for a while because I wasn't used to folding clothes that way. And even though I never finished a single blouse unless I thought I'd finally done it properly, when Mother would inspect my share of the clothes, she often said I wasn't following instructions and she would loosen out all the blouses and tell me to start over again. Sometimes I sat there for hours going over the folding repeatedly because she wasn't satisfied. Both sisters Rachel and Abigail once offered to show me or help with my share, but Mother refused. She told me that I had to put in the appropriate effort to learn just like everyone else was able to learn and that no exceptions would be made for me," Anna explained.

"How did that make you feel?" Kenna asked.

Anna paused for a moment then replied, "At first, I thought she was just picking on me maybe because she might not have liked me, but when I thought about it some more, I figured she was right in that just how everyone else was able to catch on, I should be able to as well. Mother was a perfectionist and one of the issues I always had with myself was not being as organized as I should be and not necessarily paying attention to detail. I realized that God must have put Mother into my life to teach me to be more excellent in my ways instead of mediocre. I actually learned to appreciate her for that."

It was evident from the expression on Kenna's face that she didn't expect that explanation. "So, you would describe your relationship with Mother Elizabeth as what?" she asked.

"I would describe it as a peaceful one which was what I aimed for," Anna said. "The first couple of months here were very difficult for me and I even questioned my calling. But eventually, I learned to do things the way she expected and after that, we had a rather quiet relationship. I respected her greatly and felt that beneath her tough exterior was a woman with a tender and caring heart. That's what I chose to believe."

Father Joe was moved by Anna's statement. He, too, shared the same sentiments about Mother Elizabeth. The archbishop was silently digesting the information.

"You were the one to find Mother Elizabeth's body," Kenna said. "Please recap what happened."

"Sister Angelica here asked me to check on Mother. Some mornings she stayed in bed much later than the rest of us did, and during those times, one of us would check on her to see if she needed anything."

"Uh—huh…" Kenna was nodding.

"Well, when I got to her room," Anna continued, "I found her on the floor with a knife in her chest."

"What did you do?" Detective Jackson asked her.

"I panicked and screamed, then on reflex, I pulled the knife out. Looking back now, I wish

I hadn't done that, but in my mind…the knife didn't belong there. And Mother certainly didn't belong on that floor in a pool of blood!"

The room was silent as Anna recounted the events of that morning—the reason for them being there in that moment.

"When my fellow sisters came to see what had happened, Sister Gertrude found a plastic bag on the dresser and that's where I put the knife, which she then handed over to Detective Wally."

"Yes, I know. Thank you, Sister," Kenna replied.

She then turned to Rosa Perez.

"Sister Perez, would you please share what type of relationship you had with Mother Elizabeth Rhinehart?"

Rosa sighed, and at that moment, tears gushed from her eyes. "I'm sorry! I'm sorry!" She shook her head, frantically.

"Do you need a moment?" Kenna asked.

"No. I'm fine." She dabbed her eyes with the balled-up tissue she was holding. "I know I'm supposed to be truthful here—not because I'm being questioned by the police, but because

God is watching and that's what I care about the most."

The room was deathly quiet as everyone, especially her fellow sisters, were dying to hear how she would answer that question. "I first met Mother Superior twenty-two years ago when I entered this convent as an aspirant. At that time, she welcomed me with open arms, and although she had a stern way about her back then, she also had a warmth that you could feel as she was very energetic and passionate about doing things that would benefit God's kingdom. It was her idea to establish a bookstore on these premises—one of her many projects. She took me by the hand and taught me a lot of things about my role as a nun and about life in general. I'll never forget how good I felt being in her presence and as Anna indicated, she was a perfectionist, and I too, agree that being in Mother's presence demanded more structure on our part." She paused for a moment, then continued. "Laziness was something she never tolerated and even though I had quite a lazy streak in those days, I straightened up fairly quickly after I got here."

Her last comment forced a smile upon many of their faces.

"However, over the past several years, I've noticed a dramatic switch in Mother's personality. I assumed her various health issues that showed up within the past twelve years or so might have caused her to be more impatient than she was before. She became much more impatient, even belligerent…"

"How often would you say?" Sam Jackson asked.

"On a daily basis. It's like she became a different person gradually over time to the extent that I never wanted to be in the same room with her anymore because she constantly griped about everything. One time, after she got angry at me for something I can't remember anymore since it's been so long ago—she told me that I had wasted my life being a nun and that it was not my calling and never was."

"She said that?" Kenna was shocked.

"Yes." Rosa nodded. "Well, that time, I didn't hold my tongue like I usually did, and I told her she didn't have the right to say such an awful thing to me and that I was no longer going to put up with her disrespect. She then told me some things I would not repeat."

"This is an interrogation, Sister Perez, so you would need to be completely forthcoming with us," Sam Jackson said.

"She said I was fat and ugly, and that's the only reason I ever came here to begin with," Rosa continued. "I always weighed around one hundred and forty pounds for most of my adulthood; I hardly think that's obese. But when I saw she resorted to name-calling, I decided I would not respond to that and instead, I contacted the office of the archbishop and left a complaint with his secretary."

All eyes were now on Archbishop Simms.

"Did you receive such a complaint about Mother Elizabeth Rhinehart, Your Excellency?" Kenna asked him.

He cleared his throat. "Yes, I did."

"And what did you do?"

"I called Mother Elizabeth to a meeting at my office and I discussed Sister Rosa's complaint with her. She admitted that she had said those things to Sister Rosa and also that she was within reason," he added.

"Within reason?" Kenna grimaced.

"Yes. In essence, she defended her actions and said that Sister Rosa was at fault and everyone who'd complained about her."

"So, there were other complaints?"

"Yes, there were—many over the past few years."

"From whom?" Kenna probed.

"Some of the nuns at the convent; others were parishioners, and a few were people she'd run into at the market or even the gas station. Most of the complaints were similar where she was accused of being belligerent or rude."

He went on to explain how he asked her to retire and she refused.

"She was eighty-two-years-old and I realize we had looked the other way for a long time regarding her behavior."

A few moments of silence ensued and Kenna allowed Rosa to conclude her statement.

"So, in a nutshell, you would say that you and Mother Elizabeth had a bad relationship?" Kenna asked.

Rosa hesitated for a moment, then said, "Yes. I feel terrible admitting this, but for a long time, especially after that incident, I hated her and even wished she were dead."

There was a collective gasp inside the room.

"But after much prayer and seeking God's face through fasting, I asked for God's forgiveness and I left her to Him." She glanced around the room. "With all that said, I didn't kill her. The thought never crossed my mind and never would have because I don't have it in me."

Father Joe's ears were stinging with shock. He had no idea that Mother Elizabeth had gotten on this nun's last nerve that she actually wanted her to drop dead. He leaned over and asked the archbishop if he would like a drink of water because he surely needed one. Then he excused himself from the room, easing the door shut behind him and headed for the kitchen.

As he walked, he pondered the revelations in the room thus far and felt terrible that one person could have caused so much strife and heartache. Someone who was supposed to be a good example to others and to uplift and inspire them like Mother Elizabeth had once done for him.

He knew he was being watched closely by police officers as he went to the kitchen and poured the water. Joe had no issues with it since he knew how serious it was for a crime scene to be contaminated.

He returned to the conference room a few minutes later and handed Simms a glass of cold water.

"Thank you, Father," Simms said, quietly.

"You're welcome."

Sister Sarah Robinson was currently being questioned.

"Being the eldest amongst my sisters, I always try to be a source of peace to everyone," she uttered in a shaky voice. "Even to Mother Elizabeth who was three years younger than I am."

Kenna nodded slowly.

"I know that what Sister Rosa said in terms of her feelings might've sounded so terrible, but I don't think we ought to judge her for her feelings. After all, she was just being truthful."

"I appreciate that, Sister Sarah, but please answer the question about what type of relationship you had with Mother Superior," Kenna said.

"She and I never quarreled—not once in all the years I've been here. It's not that we never had the opportunity! Much to the contrary. I would say that I always tended to see the good in people even though it may be difficult sometimes, and I was never one for quarrelling. So, if something didn't go my way, I accepted it as God's will and I focused my energy on something else that was positive and uplifting. Mother Elizabeth was a hard woman, but she was a good woman and I loved her. And already, I miss her. She brought structure and order to this place, and everywhere she went, she demanded the same. Sometimes that angered people, but not me. Like I said, I choose to see the good in people and that's why she and I could have good chats and sip tea on the porch after Mass some evenings and got along quite well. I do admit that I am one of the few people I've seen who had a fairly peaceful relationship with her, but that's probably because I always relented when it came to her. I never contended with her and certainly was not going to lose my peace over another human being. I hope I finally answered your question."

"You have." Kenna smiled.

Angelica was asked to go next and she seemed eager to get it over with.

"Mother Elizabeth and I had a cordial relationship, for the most part," she said.

"For the most part?" Jackson asked her.

"Yes. Like some here have already indicated, it was only within the last decade or so that Mother seemed to have changed in terms of being grumpy and difficult to deal with, and to talk to. I agree that she was always quite stern, but with that was a generally pleasant person many years ago. However, even though she clearly became more hot-tempered, she and I got along fine. I was sometimes able to calm her when she got really upset about something by showing that it wasn't as big of a deal as she'd thought. On a few occasions, I saw the *old her* emerge, but just for a split second. Maybe it was all those pills the doctors had prescribed for her conditions that changed her because the real Mother Elizabeth was not all that bad."

"Is that all you want to add?" Kenna asked.

"Yes, that's all," Rosa replied.

Claire Hans, the sixty-year-old nun, was clearly nervous as she anticipated being called upon next.

"This is all very unsettling," she said. "Who would've thought we'd all be sitting here at this table having such a dreadful conversation!"

"Just take a deep breath, Sister Claire," Joe said from his chair. "It's going to be all right."

"Thank you, Father," she replied, gratefully. She did as he instructed and felt a bit more relaxed.

Claire Hans, from Joe's recollection, had a nervous streak for quite some time. It was only after she'd entered perimenopause that anxiety had apparently latched on to her, and after coming out on the other side, the anxiety lessened, but never left completely.

"Are you okay?" Kenna asked.

"Yes, I'm okay." She took in another deep breath, then exhaled.

"I was afraid of Mother Elizabeth and at the same time I revered her," she said. "She reminded me of a very strong man…"

"A strong *man*?" Kenna grimaced.

"Yes, she did. Well, she was pretty heavy and had quite a domineering demeanor that I was so afraid to cross her. So, I stayed out of her way as much as possible and did everything she wanted me to do—how she wanted me to do it."

"So, you never had any run-ins with her?" Kenna probed.

"Well…not *run-ins*, but just like mostly everyone else, I was reprimanded for something or the other quite often."

"You didn't resent her?"

"*Resent* her? No! I was too afraid of her for that. She was like the father I never had."

Father Joe was shaking his head. He always said there was only one Claire Hans.

Kenna clearly recognized that one needed some sort of therapy and promptly wrapped up her questioning of her. Each of the other nuns who subsequently gave their statements expressed the difficulty and tension in the convent under Mother Elizabeth's leadership: Martha Wingate, Marianne Petersen, Ruth

Harman, Pleasant Chin, Hannah Bowleg, Esther Shehogobin, Rachel Wright and Abigail Fairchild. Their ages ranged between twenty-seven and forty-nine. Sister Gertrude was last to be questioned and as expected by all who knew her, her expression was stoic and her speech highly confident.

"Mother Elizabeth was not a nice person," she started. "She was arrogant, self-centered, obnoxious, overbearing, accusatory and critical to the utmost extreme."

At the sound of those words, the archbishop looked at Father Joe with a mixture of surprise and disgust rolled into one.

"She was a terrible woman!" Gertrude continued. "And I avoided her like a plague whenever I possibly could. She made all of our lives miserable and I'm only one of the few here bold enough to say it. I will admit that when we discovered her body, I was not too surprised as I knew that sooner or later, she would cross the wrong person and that they might act on impulse."

Kenna leaned in, admiring this nun's apparent brutal honesty. "So, I take it that you two didn't have a good relationship at all…" she said.

"Not in the slightest—especially after she accused me seven years ago of misappropriating funds while I performed administrative duties which included the bookkeeping—without any supporting evidence whatsoever. How any such thing could've possibly come to her mind baffles me to this day. She dragged my name through the mud, called me a thief and turned over the bookkeeping duties to Sister Esther. She made me look like a fool and I still don't appreciate it! Back then, if I hadn't gone down on my knees for her, the devil might've convinced *me* to kill her!"

The archbishop was beside himself with shock over Gertrude's stinging admission.

"Has she lost her mind?" He leaned over and whispered to Joe.

"I would be surprised if none of them had, considering how Mother has obviously driven them up the wall and for so long," Joe replied.

Feeling partially responsible for their suffering, Simms did not respond.

"Do you have any ideas about who might've been responsible for Mother Elizabeth's death?" Kenna asked Gertrude.

Gertrude looked around the room at her fellow nuns, then said, "I haven't the slightest clue. It could've been anybody."

"Thank you, Sister," Kenna leaned back. "Well, before we wrap up here for now, I would like to ask all of you that same question. Do you have any idea who might've been responsible for Mother Elizabeth Rhinehart's death?"

In addition to shaking of heads, the answer was a collective *No*.

"Okay then. Since your living quarters is currently a crime scene, you would need to find somewhere else to stay until we can turn the property back over to you," Kenna told them.

"That won't be a problem, Detective," Archbishop Simms noted. "We have a monastery nearby on Ructus Hill. A good portion of it is unoccupied, so our sisters will stay there until further notice."

"Perfect! We know where to find everyone if we need to."

Simms called his office and made arrangements for the nuns' temporary sleeping quarters. They all had cars of their own and would soon make their way, along with some of their belongings, to Ructus Hill.

"Thank you, Detective, for allowing us to stay for the questioning," Joe told Wally Profado, who'd allowed his junior, but seasoned detectives to conduct the interrogation.

"Don't mention it," Wally said.

"Would you please keep my office updated regarding the investigation?" Simms asked.

"Definitely, Your Excellency," he replied.

ive days later…

Joe was jolted from a deep sleep when the phone rang.

"Who could this be so early?" he muttered, glancing at his desk clock which flashed the time: *6:20 A.M.* He reached over to the nightstand, switched on the lamp, then answered the phone, "Morning. Father Joe here."

"Father, it's Sue! They've arrested Mike for Mother Elizabeth's murder!"

She was in tears and beside herself.

"What? How can that be?" Joe sat straight up in bed.

"I don't know," she replied. "I'm on the road now following them to the Cylon Street police station."

"I'll be right there."

Joe couldn't believe his ears and squinted his eyes to figure out if he was in a dream or not.

The pinch he gave himself was the prevalent factor that proved he was wide awake.

In five minutes, he was dressed and heading out the door. As he drove to the police station, he was praying that it was all just a foolish mistake.

On arrival there, he found Sue sitting in the lobby with the most terrified look he'd ever seen on her face.

"Father!" She ran to him the moment he walked through the door and hugged him tightly. "I don't know how they could do this! Mike is innocent!"

"I know, dear. I'm sure it's a mistake and they'll realize that soon enough," Joe replied.

He headed over to the reception counter where a policeman had been stationed.

"Good morning. I'd like to see Detective Wally Profado if he's on," Joe said.

"He's here, but busy," the officer replied, nonchalantly. "You can wait over there if you want, but I can't say how long he's gonna be."

"However long it takes, I'll be here."

Joe and Sue started to walk off.

"Excuse me, sir," the officer said. "What's your name?"

Joe looked back. "Father Joe McCullen."

The officer nodded, then jotted the name onto the register.

"This is unbelievable!" Sue exclaimed as they sat down together.

It was quiet in the station that Thursday morning. No one else was in the lobby and Joe took it as a sign that all was still generally well in Old Providence, especially after the new chief of police was sworn in four years earlier. Dwight Reddington was his name; they used to be close friends back in middle school.

"What did they tell you?" Joe asked Sue.

"You mean after they barged into our house and dragged Mike out of his bed?"

Her revelation broke his heart. "Yep."

"They read him his rights and said he was being arrested for Mother Elizabeth Rhinehart's murder. That's all they said and I couldn't get them to tell me anything more."

"Don't worry." He patted her hand. "We'll get to the bottom of this and Mike will be home in no time."

Sue found Joe's confidence reassuring and only hoped and prayed that he was right.

* * * *

9:10 A.M.

"Have you heard the dreadful news?" Virginia Adams asked Kate Brown.

Both women worked in the church office; Virginia, thirty-nine years old, took care of the accounting and Kate, six years her junior, was a data entry clerk. They'd been employed at the parish for nine years; both hired within the same week.

"What news?" Kate asked.

"Mike Tenney was arrested for Mother Elizabeth's murder!"

"You're kidding!"

Virginia quickly shook her head. "Nope. I'm as serious as a heart attack."

"Gosh! Do you really think Mike could be responsible?"

"Why not? We all heard about how Mother Elizabeth ranted about him last week when he was working over there at the convent,"

Virginia stated. "She told everyone she could that he's nothing but a leech and how he was using Father Joe for his money. Mike didn't take too kindly to that. We all know that nothing's a secret around here."

"Yeah, but Mike is a pretty decent guy, Virginia. Being upset over how Mother Elizabeth talked about him and deciding to *murder* her are two completely different things," Kate noted. "I just don't believe it."

Virginia always hated Kate's optimism. She thought it made her the worse type of person to gossip to, but Virginia was stuck with her since they sat only a few feet away from each other in the tiny church office. Agatha Hall was there—the fifty-nine-year-old administrator— and so was Sue McCloud, Father Joe's secretary. But neither one of those women seemed to have anything in common with her and Kate. At least, that's how Virginia felt.

"Well, I'm not one to swear for anybody," Virginia stated. "Sometimes, people we least expect to do certain things are the ones guilty of the most heinous crimes."

Kate noticed she was getting annoyed and knew it was because she didn't happen to agree with her. "I suppose you're right," she quietly said.

"I'm sure that I am, but time will tell anyway."

Kate proceeded to key items into her computer and hoped that Virginia would soon get the message that she was no longer interested in the topic.

* * * *

9:21 A.M.

"Father Joe…good morning! Please come this way," Wally Profado said upon entering the lobby.

"Sure!" Joe answered.

He and Sue got up immediately and followed Wally through a side door next to the reception counter.

"I hope you weren't waiting for too long."

"You're here now and that's all that matters," Joe replied.

Sue attempted to get information on Mike's arrest while they waited for two hours in the lobby, but she was not assisted. They were advised to wait for Wally Profado.

Wally gestured for them to have a seat in his office.

"Sue…" he started as she walked past him at the door.

She took a seat, then said, "I want to know why you all have arrested Mike."

Wally calmly headed to his chair and sat down.

"You know Mike couldn't have possibly killed Mother Elizabeth, Wally!" Sue added.

"We don't know that," Wally answered, staring her in the face.

"He's been raised in the church and under the guidance of Father Joe, for goodness' sake! He couldn't have had a better example in his life on how to be a good, productive citizen."

"I agree with you there, but like many children who were exposed to admirable habits and had good examples, some fall away and do things that go against everything they've been taught. You cannot swear for your child, Susan. It's just that simple."

Joe cleared his throat and raised his hand. "Okay. Now, that all the opinions have been placed on the table, let's get to the facts. Shall we? What do you have, Wally? I presume it must be something concrete since you all have arrested Mike."

Wally quickly nodded. "I want you to know, Father, that if I thought for a moment that Mike was innocent, he never would've been brought here."

"That's baloney!" Sue snarled. "You and I both know that you resent me for turning you down when you were making advances toward me years ago and I reported your no-good behind to Father Joe!"

"That's ludicrous!" Wally grinned. "You made the whole thing up."

"You know I didn't! That's why they stopped you from ushering because you couldn't keep your hands off my behind when we went inside the office to put up the money! You're a pervert! And because I exposed you for who you are, you had it in for me and are now using Mother Elizabeth's death to get back at me by targeting Mike. But the devil is a liar! You will reap what you sow, Wally Profado!"

"Settle down, people. Settle down!" Joe said. "How can we ever get to the bottom of this matter if you two are gonna be bickering back and forth? Mike doesn't need this foolishness and neither do I. I was already deprived of at least an hour's sleep this morning because of what happened to him. So, again…I ask for the facts." He was now looking at Wally.

Wally sighed heavily. "You're right, Father, and I apologize. We received a confidential call a few days ago from someone who implicated Mike Tenney in Mother Elizabeth Rhinehart's death. The caller expressed that she heard him threaten Mother when they were having an argument on the lawn a week ago."

"Threatened her like how?" Sue insisted, still fighting with everything inside of her to keep her cool.

"The caller reportedly said that Mother was adamant about telling Father Joe that he needed to stop letting him and you—Sue—leech off of him and that she was going to tell everyone she knew that he was nothing but a user, an opportunist and a bum. In turn, Mike allegedly threatened to kill her if she went and spread lies about him."

"Who made these allegations?" Joe asked him.

"I'm afraid, that's confidential, Father."

"You're telling me that a person can call the police and accuse another of a crime such as this and conveniently hide in the shadows?" Joe returned. "Are we referring to a mob-related hit here or not?"

Sue was nodding. "I'd like to know too!"

"Wouldn't that person have to testify in court to this assertion?" Joe continued.

"Yes, they would," Wally replied.

"So, why is their identity a secret now?"

Wally seemed momentarily at a loss for words.

"Cat's got your tongue, Wally?" Sue pursed her lips. "You know—this whole thing is stupid because it shows us that someone can make an accusation against you Father, me and anyone else and these bumbling idiots on the police force would be dumb enough to come and arrest us without any solid proof or justification! Is this what justice looks like in this town? If so, decent folk like us need to move out or trashy officers like Wally Profado and company need to be the ones to get lost!"

"That's enough! I've had it!" Wally stood up abruptly. "You get out of my office, Sue, or I'll drag you out!"

Joe immediately stood up and so did Sue.

"You drag me out if you think you're big and bad!" Sue replied. "Touch me and I'll put my Christianity aside for just one minute!"

"Everyone, calm down!" Joe raised his hands. "This is not how Christians are supposed to behave." He turned to Sue. "I know this is a difficult situation for you, and it is for me too, but you must get a hold of yourself. All of this name-calling and criticizing is not going to help Mike—and he needs to be our focus."

She sighed deeply. "You're right, Father. I apologize for my behavior, but I'm just so upset!" Her eyes started to well with tears.

"I know you are, but it's going to be all right. We just need to sit down, discuss the facts and then we can move forward from there."

"Okay," she said.

"Are we good now?" He asked Wally.

Wally slowly nodded and they all sat down again.

"As I said," he continued. "Right now, I cannot reveal the identity of the caller. Until we have directives from the chief, there is certain information we cannot disclose publicly."

"I understand…" Joe replied, "…but I don't agree. Be that as it may… is that the sole basis for Mike's detainment?"

Sue was sobbing quietly, wiping her eyes with the sleeve of her blouse. Wally glanced over at her a couple of times, but seemed unfazed.

"Actually, we're building a case and I have to admit that it doesn't look good for Mike," he told Joe. "Let me say first and foremost that I have nothing against this kid. He's served the church ever since he was a child. He's an altar boy; helps around the church grounds using skills he learned from the maintenance crew and others, and I, personally, always liked him. The last thing I would want to do with a seventeen-year-old kid is to get him locked up for a crime he didn't commit. But as difficult as this is for anyone to hear, the kid obviously has problems that were either overlooked or just haven't been dealt with. I'm not blaming you, Father Joe, but the facts cannot be denied."

"What on earth are you talking about, Wally?" Sue asked. If the glare in her eyes was a knife, he would've been cut into a million pieces.

Wally stretched out his arms on the desk and interlaced his fingers. "We spoke with the guidance counselor at Mike's school who indicated that he was suspended just before school closed for the summer for beating up another kid. Are you aware of that, Sue?"

"Of course, I'm aware of it!"

"Well, I wasn't," Joe interjected. "What was this about?"

"Mike said the kid, who's also in his class, always made snide remarks about him being *nobody's kid* because neither of his biological parents are in his life," Sue explained. "Despite the fact that's it's common knowledge that his mother is deceased. He said he was already feeling a bit down that day because he hadn't done very well on a couple of his final exams and you know, Father, his whole goal is to get scholarship offers to play softball…"

"Yes!" Joe nodded quickly.

"Well, that kid messed with him on a bad day and Mike naturally reacted. I would never condone him hurting another student or anyone, for that matter, but none of us are perfect. Any one of us could've flipped if we had been pushed hard enough and as frequently as that kid pushed Mike."

"Violence is unacceptable, no matter what," Wally responded.

Joe noticed that Sue was about to let loose on him again and quickly intervened. "It's okay, Sue. Just relax," he told her.

Sue was a godly woman, by most accounts, but everyone who knew her knew that she would turn the world upside down for Mike Tenney. She had dedicated her entire life to his welfare and would fight tooth and nail to protect him. What she wanted so badly to do to Wally Profado that morning was something she wouldn't describe to a living soul, especially to Father Joe.

"I'm fine, Father," she replied. "The Bible says to resist the devil and he will flee. So, I'm resisting."

Joe turned Wally's way again. "So, Mike had a fight and got suspended. Is that all to your case—those two things you mentioned?" he asked, calmly.

"No—there's one more thing," Wally said.

"And that is…" Joe waited patiently.

"It's been alleged that Mike had another issue with Mother Elizabeth, apart from that of last week."

Confused, Joe looked at Sue, then back at Wally. "Another issue?"

"Yes," Wally answered.

"I'm not aware of any other issue he had with Mother Elizabeth," Sue said.

"We've been informed that Mike was getting a bit too close to one of the nuns there by the name of Anna Gunter and Mother Elizabeth reprimanded both of them for it."

"I've never heard of such a thing!" Sue barked.

"Neither have I," Joe said. "And knowing Mother Elizabeth, if that was in fact true, she wouldn't have kept it to herself, by any means."

"That's what I thought when we got the news. I certainly hadn't heard anything about it prior to this," Wally admitted. "So, we made a trip to Ructus Hill and questioned Sister Anna and she confirmed the whole incident."

"I can't believe this," Sue muttered. "Mike and I have a great relationship; he doesn't hide anything from me." She looked at Wally. "I need to speak with him, and I need to know how long you people plan on keeping him here."

"Mike will be arraigned tomorrow morning at ten o'clock. Because of the brutality of the crime and the fact that the victim was a nun, it was agreed that he will be tried as an adult."

"I bet you agreed to that!" Sue blurted.

"You can get an attorney to represent him during the arraignment or a court-appointed attorney will be provided," he said, ignoring her last statement.

"Forget the court-appointed attorney," Joe said. "We'll get Jim Cruz to take the case."

"Smart choice." Wally nodded.

"To think my boy will have to stay in this godforsaken place for I don't know how long!" Sue exclaimed.

"Mike will be transported to the town's juvenile facility in Maiklen until he either gets bail or goes to trial. We can't put him with hardened criminals since he's underage."

"But you'll have him tried as an adult!" Sue said, angrily.

"That was not my choice, Sue. I don't run the justice system. That falls in the hand of the district attorney's office."

A few moments of awkward silence ensued.

"Look…I know what we have is all circumstantial evidence, but by the same token, such evidence has been responsible for many trial convictions, and you must be prepared for that. Even though I know it looks bad for Mike, I'm hoping that this department has it all wrong and it would be proven in court. In the meanwhile, it's incumbent upon me to advise you both of the possibility that he may or may not be granted bail tomorrow. Just so you know…"

"Thank you, Wally," Joe stood to his feet. "We'd like to see the boy now if you don't mind."

"Sure," Wally stood up as well. "Right this way."

ike Tenney was being detained in a six by nine-foot cell. His face lit up when he saw them approaching; they looked like angels to him.

Wally unlocked the bars and allowed Joe and Sue inside.

Sue quickly hugged Mike and neither of them wanted to let go of the other. She was in tears, but Mike was holding strong, restraining the floodgates of emotions that wanted desperately to escape, just as he desperately craved his own freedom.

"I'm so sorry you're going through this, son," Sue told him. "I know you're innocent."

"Thanks, Mom," he said, as they parted.

Joe hugged him next and patted his back. "This too shall pass," Joe said. "How are you holding up?"

"Okay, I guess."

Joe noticed the look of concern on the boy's face, but he also knew that Mike was a strong kid and was the least person he expected to break when the current circumstances warranted it. No one was going to think they'd gotten the best of him. It was Mike's mentality—the fortress he'd built around his emotions due to the pain of having both biological parents absent from his life. Joe had talked to him a few times about not being afraid to feel vulnerable and that everything was not within one's control, but he knew despite Mike's agreement to the idea, the boy still struggled to come to terms with it.

"I must ask you a question, Mike, and it may sound strange coming from me…but I will ask anyway," Joe said.

"I didn't do it, Father. I didn't kill Mother Elizabeth," Mike immediately expressed. "You know I was raised better than that. I did hit that punk kid in school and I might've been a bit too friendly with Sister Anna, much to Mother Elizabeth's displeasure, but I can swear on my mother's grave that I don't have any romantic feelings for Sister Anna and I didn't kill anyone."

"Don't you dare swear, Michael Alphonso Tenney!" Sue set him straight.

"Sorry," he replied.

"What about the threat?" Joe asked.

"What threat? What are you talking about?" Mike frowned.

"Someone told the police that they heard you threaten Mother Elizabeth when you two had that issue a week ago."

Mike's eyes widened. "That's a lie! I'd never do such a thing! I told you guys exactly how that incident went and threatening her wasn't anywhere in my vocabulary. What do I look like? Whoever said that is damn liar!"

"I know you're upset, Mike, but you watch your mouth," Sue warned him without batting an eye.

"You've gotta believe me that I'm no murderer, Father!" he insisted.

"I do believe you, son," Joe said. "The real killer is still out there and I'm gonna find out who that is."

"You're being arraigned tomorrow and Father is going to speak with Jim Cruz from church to represent you," Sue added.

"Okay." The boy nodded. "Mister Cruz has a reputation around here for being a saint in the sanctuary and a bulldog in the courtroom."

Joe and Sue both smiled.

'He's a fighter, all right," Joe agreed. "The best man to have in your corner when you find yourself in a hot mess."

Mike saw the worry in his mother's eyes and put his arm across her shoulder. "I'm sorry I'm putting you through all this, Mom. You don't need this stress with your high blood pressure and all…"

Sue quickly cupped his face. "None of this is your fault, Mike, so you have nothing to apologize for. Remember how you always said you want to be an attorney someday and how you'll do pro bono work for people unjustly accused?"

He nodded.

"Well. Maybe the good Lord is allowing this to happen so you'll know firsthand what it's like and you'll be a better fighter in the courtroom for people who otherwise couldn't afford good representation."

"I think you're right, Mom. What do you think, Father?"

"I wholeheartedly agree with your mother. Something good always comes out of something bad when the person it happens to trusts in The Lord. I've seen it happen countless times and this time is no exception. I'm praying for you, son. Just stand firm and stay strong, ya hear?"

"I hear you, Father." Mike smiled.

He embraced them once more before they left and his heart ached as he watched his adoptive mother leave, her face drenched in tears.

* * * *

"I told Mike and now I'm telling you, Sue: stand firm and stay strong. That boy needs your strength," Joe said as he walked her to her car.

"Okay." She dried her tears. "I just can't believe this is happening!" She started sobbing again.

He tried to console her. "I know. I can't tell you what it's doing to me inside, but I know that right now our feelings don't matter. Mike's the one incarcerated and facing serious jail time for Mother Elizabeth's death. We must keep our minds focused so that anything at all that could possibly be helpful to his case can get through."

"You're right, Father." She dried her tears again.

They arrived at her blue 2008 Honda.

"So, I'm going to contact Jim Cruz and arrange for him to have a meeting with us at the rectory as soon as he can, and we'll go from there."

"It's a start," Sue said.

"Yes, but for now, let's pray together for God to guide all involved every step of the way."

Sue was confused. "You mean…we should pray right here…in the parking lot?"

"God is everywhere, dear. Did you think He could be everywhere else except the police station's parking lot?"

"No." She managed a chuckle. "Okay, let's pray then."

They bowed their heads as Joe prayed for direction and strength.

"Thank you, Father," Sue told him afterwards.

"Thanks be to God. Go and get freshened up, and I'll see you at the office in an hour." He started to walk off in the direction of his car.

"But Father…"

"No *buts*, Sue. You're not going home alone to mope around the house. At least at work you'll have the support you need even if all you can do is sit quietly. And whenever you're ready to go—just leave."

"Okay. I'll be there."

"Good choice."

* * * *

"Good morning, everyone," Sue said, upon entering the church office. Virginia Adams and Kate Brown were there alone since Agatha had called in sick.

"Sue! Oh my gosh, I heard the dreadful news!" Virginia got up and hurried over to her the moment she walked through the door. "Please, let me take your bag."

Sue reluctantly handed it to her.

"How is Mikey? He must be terrified."

"As good as expected, considering the circumstances." Sue made her way over to her desk and sat down.

"How could anyone possibly think that Mikey could be involved in Mother Elizabeth's murder? It's unfathomable!"

"Same thing I'm thinking.," Sue retrieved some files from her desk drawer and rested them on the desk.

"So, what did the cops say? Why do they suspect that he had anything to do with it?" Virginia probed. "Oh, wait! Does it have anything to do with that most upsetting incident last week?" She placed a finger on her chin.

"I really can't say, Virginia. Nothing is very clear at this point, but we have an attorney who's going to get to the bottom of it. Now, if you don't mind, I'd better get to work."

Virginia turned to leave, then stopped in her tracks. "By the way…what are you even doing here? I didn't expect you to come in today."

"I'm here because I have work to do, Virginia, and if need be, I can be reached whether I'm home or here."

"I see. Okay, then. Just so you know, I'm praying for you and Mikey."

"Thanks. We appreciate that."

As she rounded the bend near her desk, Virginia arched her brows at Kate with a smug grin on her face.

"Did you hear that?" She spoke quietly after sitting down.

Kate nodded.

"She's pathetic. Doesn't know a thing about mothering."

"Why do you say that?" Kate was surprised.

"Because her son's sitting in jail and she's here working! Can you believe that?"

"It's only her and Mikey, Virginia. Maybe she needs to be around other people and maybe working will keep her sane. She must be terribly worried."

"Well, I don't think she's acting like that." Virginia squirted some hand sanitizer on her hand from a bottle nearby. She was diagnosed with OCD as a child and believed that germs were practically everywhere. The thought of countless germs being on Sue's bag she'd voluntarily carried repulsed her, and she couldn't wait to rid herself of the filth.

"I'm really sorry about Mike," Kate told Sue, minutes later, while she was on her way to the restroom. "Thanks, Kate," Sue replied.

"Just know that people care and I'm here for you if you ever wanna talk or just need a shoulder to cry on. That's all I wanted to say."

"I appreciate that," Sue responded gratefully.

Kate continued on to the restroom and Sue gazed at her computer screen. Mike was all she could think about. Her eyes drifted to a desktop plaque Mike's mother had given her twenty years earlier which read: *Believe the incredible and you can do the impossible.* She knew them to be the words of a beloved priest who was charismatic and wise, and served as a great inspiration to many.

"Believe the incredible and you can do the impossible," she whispered. "It doesn't matter how things look if I believe for a complete turnaround," she sought to convince herself. "It's called *faith*—that's it in a nutshell."

She closed her eyes and uttered a silent prayer, then read those words again. "I do believe," she said quietly. "I do believe."

Just then, the phone rang and she reached over and answered it.

"Jim returned a voice note to me," Joe said. "He'll be here at the rectory this afternoon and will call when he's on his way."

"Thanks, Father," she replied.

"Staying strong?"

"Yes, I am. Staying strong."

"Okay, good. I'll be off in a few minutes to make my rounds at the hospital. Will be back by lunch time."

_____

6

*A*fter Joe opened the door of the rectory for him later that afternoon, Jim Cruz could tell that Sue McCloud was carrying the weight of the world on her shoulders as she sat there in the living room.

"I came as soon as I could." Jim took a seat. "I was in court practically all day, but after I got your message, Father, I decided to swing by and pay Mike a visit."

"You did?" Sue asked.

"I did. He and I spoke in detail."

"That's good," Joe said.

Jim shifted in his chair, now facing Sue.

"Mike is a strong kid and I know he's an honest one," he said. "I can bet my bottom dollar that he's a scapegoat for the real killer."

"Exactly what I thought!" Sue replied, emphatically.

"Apart from getting him bail tomorrow, my job will be to subsequently create reasonable doubt in the minds of the jurors during the trial because it's clearly unadvisable for him to plead guilty to this crime."

"And *my* job will be to dig deeply to find out who set this young man up!" Joe exclaimed. "Whomever it is will have to contend with me."

"Me too!" Sue added.

"I understand your enthusiasm Father and Sue, but please allow me and my team of investigators to take care of that part. All of it will help to create that reasonable doubt I told you about," Jim said.

"But you're talking about doing that at the trial," Joe replied. "I'm talking about getting this boy off the hook before it ever gets to trial."

"That's the job for my investigators, Father. I'm covering all bases here."

"Thanks, Jim. I hear ya, but you do you and I'll do me," Joe frankly stated.

Jim laughed. "You know—coming here, I knew this wouldn't be cut and dry."

"Smart man," Joe replied. "Smart man."

"Wait—do you have an idea of who might be the real killer?" Jim asked him, suspiciously.

"Not a clue."

Jim looked at Sue who shrugged.

"I only know who's not the killer and that's me. So, in my books, everyone else is a suspect." Joe got up to get a drink from the kitchen. "Don't be shy about the bill, Jim. I've got a few dollars saved. If your fees go beyond that, you're on your own, dear friend."

Jim laughed again and shook his head. "We'll work something out. Let's just focus on getting Mike back home and his life back to normal."

"Thank you, Jim." Sue reached over and squeezed his hand.

"I'm happy to help in any way that I can. I can only imagine what you and Mike are going through. Can't be easy."

"It's not easy," Sue replied.

Joe returned with three tall glasses of ice-cold water and handed one to each of them.

"We all need these to cool our nerves," he said, having a seat on the couch. "We're three hotheads."

Sue and Jim chuckled. Joe always managed to lighten the mood. Sometimes his facial expressions were enough to tickle someone in his presence. Despite his occasional humor, no one in his parish was more determined to get things done. And the criticism of some of his own spiritual children never managed to deter him from standing up for what he believed was right—even if he did it alone.

"We spoke with Wally this morning," Joe told Jim.

"I did too, but he was pretty tightlipped," Jim replied.

"Really?" Sue frowned.

"It was clear to me that he was only offering up the bare minimum and I found that rather suspicious, especially since he's aware that Mike's freedom is on the line here."

"He's trying to get back at me," Sue said.

"You mean—over that thing involving you two years ago?"

"Only could be. Some people hold grudges for life."

"I don't know if that's his reasoning," Joe chimed in. "Maybe there's only so much info he can offer up without putting his job at risk."

"I doubt it," Jim replied. "He's offered up more to me in other cases I've been involved in. I would've expected him to be more forthcoming when it came to Mike. He's a kid, for goodness' sake."

"Wally's a jerk! That's why his wife almost left him!" Sue exclaimed. "Who in their right mind would wanna stay married to him anyway? He's not even good looking!"

"Neither is Jim, Sue! But Trina's keeping him!" Joe said.

Jim laughed. "You're too much, Father."

"I guess I am."

"So, what do we do now?" Sue asked.

"What I said from the beginning. I'll get my PIs on the case and we'll go from there."

"Okay," she replied.

Jim shook his head, contemplatively. "If it happened this way…I don't know what Mother Elizabeth might've done to anger the person who killed her, but no matter what, she didn't deserve to die."

"I agree." Sue nodded.

"She really wasn't all that bad, you know," Joe said. "I happened to know her for the better part of twenty-five years even before I was transferred to this parish, and she truly was an inspiration to me. I believe she imparted some of her strength and wisdom when I was a young priest. I have fond memories of her and how she helped the church, always giving of herself to enhance the various programs—especially those involving women and children. She believed they were a crucial part of her life's work and she never faltered with it." He crossed his legs and leaned back a little. "I think, for the most part, she may have been misunderstood. These days, people are not exercising enough patience with one another. I guess they say they don't need to waste time trying to understand you when they've got their own heap of problems they're struggling to wrap their heads around. And believe me—I get that. Regardless, we're all in this together and we're all humanly related whether we like it or not. So, sometimes we just need to learn to accept the other person for who they are with all their flaws and allow them to navigate their way through this life the best way they know how. Not with judgmental eyes, mind you—but with those of understanding that none of us gets by without making mistakes of our own and wanting others to be forgiving of them."

"Thanks for the homily, Father," Jim said. "I didn't expect one until this coming Sunday."

Joe smiled.

"I guess what you're saying, Father..." Sue started, "...is that no matter how Mother Elizabeth came across at times, we should have been ready to forgive her since we don't know what crosses of her own she's had to bear and how she might've been struggling to carry them."

"Precisely," Joe agreed. "I'm not advocating allowing people to mistreat you, by any means. Stand up to them and let them know they hurt you. Just don't harbor hatred against them because that hatred can turn into something destructive. Unless it's for the sake of self-defense, no one has a right to take the life of another. And no one certainly has the right to allow someone else to take the fall for their own misdeed."

"So true," Sue replied.

"Well, I guess I'll be going." Jim rested his empty glass on the side table and got up. "Trina and the kids are expecting me home early for dinner this evening. Things have just started settling down for me since it's been a mad rush at the office over the past few weeks."

"Oh, my good boy…" Joe stood up as well. "Things are not settling down. They're just getting started. Let me walk you to the door."

7

Sue and Jim were at Mike's arraignment the following morning. Joe had informed them that he had an appointment and regrettably, could not be there. In the meanwhile, he was on his way to Ructus Hill for a special meeting.

"Good morning, Father," Angelica Gottlieb greeted him at the door of the monastery.

"Good morning, Sister. How are you today?" he asked.

"Just fine, Father."

They started down the hallway together.

"We're all grieving Mother's loss in our own ways," the nun stated.

"I'm sure that's the case; she will be missed."

"Yes indeed. There was only one Mother Elizabeth." She smiled. "Please…right this way. She's expecting you."

They stopped at a door at the very end of the hallway on the left. Angelica knocked once, then opened it.

"Father, it's nice to see you again," Gertrude said, rising from her desk. "When you called and said you wanted to meet with me this morning, I decided to brew a cup of black coffee for you—just the way you like it."

"You're very thoughtful, Sister."

"I'll go and get it," Angelica said, leaving the room.

Gertrude sat down again. "I would like to start off by thanking you for filling in for our chaplain, Father Brimley, while he was on vacation these past few weeks. Driving back and forth to the convent was an extra duty I'm sure you could've done without."

"It's been a pleasure," Joe said.

"So...to what do I owe this pleasure?" she asked.

"I wish to speak with you about Mother Elizabeth's death."

"I thought as much, Father, but I disclosed everything I know—*which isn't anything much, really*—during the police interrogation."

95

"Yes. Yes. But I wanted to ask you something specifically in private," he said.

Just then, Angelica returned with the coffee and rested the mug on the desk in front of him.

"Bless you, Sister," he said before she left the room, shutting the door behind them.

"Detective Kenna asked you yesterday if you had any theories about who might have wanted Mother Elizabeth dead and I don't know if it was just me who noticed, but you hesitated for a brief moment there before you answered."

"Well, that's because the question required a little more forethought than the previous ones," she replied.

"You do have theories, don't you?"

"Look Father…I know that Mike and his mother are both very important to you; you've practically taken the boy under your wing. But if you're looking to me to have any helpful insights whatsoever, I think you'll be sorely disappointed."

"I understand that you'll likely be elected as Mother Elizabeth's replacement," he noted.

She looked at him suspiciously. "Well, I've certainly put in the time and have proven my capabilities. As you know, Sister Sarah is just too old and Sister Claire, on the other hand, is battling anxiety, so neither of them would make a suitable replacement." She paused for a moment. "But what does that have to do with anything?"

"Probably nothing. Just thought I'd mention it."

"Why? Because you think there's a possibility that I murdered Mother in order to acquire her position?"

"Your words—not mine, Gertrude." He cleared his throat. "I mean…*Sister*. It's just that I think the police may look at you more intently if you were to become the next Mother Superior, that's all. They may start thinking that you had an obvious motive for wanting your predecessor dead."

"That's ludicrous!" She barked.

"And they may consider the other issue you two had concerning the embezzlement accusation."

Gertrude was looking at him intently.

"I'm just showing you how easily a person who may be innocent can appear very guilty. Mike is in a similar boat, Sister. He's just a kid trying to find his place in this world. He's not going to be perfect—none of us are. Of course, he's done some foolish things, but all of us have. I think you get what I'm saying."

She nodded quickly. "I do, Father. And you're right."

Gertrude blankly gazed past him for a second, then fixed her eyes on him and said, "I personally believe one of the sisters might have done it."

Joe inwardly cringed at the sound of those words.

"There was clearly not a break-in, Father, and the convent wasn't robbed. And I'm sure you would've gathered from the interrogation that very few of us were fond of her. It sounds terrible, but life is full of surprises."

"Who stands out to you?" Joe asked.

"Well, of course, Sister Anna found the body, so in my books, she's suspect *number one*. Then second on the list of my suspects is Sister Rosa. She was the first nun to make a formal complaint about Mother Elizabeth, only to seemingly have it fall upon deaf ears.

"But why now?" Joe wondered. "Why would the killer strike *now*? The incident Sister

Rosa mentioned happened a few years ago and Sister Anna's new. So, unless she's just a bad seed, the timing doesn't make sense to me."

"Hmmm." She looked at him curiously. "What are you thinking, Father?"

"I'm thinking that whoever killed Mother Elizabeth might have used her and Mike's disagreement to get rid of her and frame him for it. That way, they figured they'd be in the clear."

So, you also suspect that one of the nuns is responsible?"

"It certainly appears possible, but someone outside the convent might've watched the drama between them that day and could've decided the same thing. Do you know of anyone Mother may have upset or offended in the neighborhood, specifically?" he asked.

"Old Charlie Mullings and a few others who came by quite regularly for food items," Gertrude said. "Charlie lives just down the street in a house he'd inherited from his grandma, but he can't afford to keep the place halfway decent since he's not working. After about his fourth visit at the convent, Mother asked him if he was looking for work. She called him a healthy, strapping man who should not have to be showing up every week for handouts and that he was cutting someone else out who really needed the assistance. Well…" She straightened up in her chair, "…Old Charlie didn't take kindly to that. He was poor, all right, but he had his pride. He broke down right then and there, and told her the last thing he ever wanted was to depend on others to eat. He said she should try losing her entire family and all of her life's savings through a divorce and see how easily she'd bounce back. I did some digging and Old Charlie used to be some Wall Street executive making a ton of money. He had a big house, fancy cars and about a couple hundred grand in the bank. Then one day, his wife told him she wanted a divorce. She moved out, took the kids, emptied their joint bank accounts leaving him penniless and the only thing she left him with was the huge mortgage over his head. He could've paid it, just like he always did, but her walking out and him losing everyone he loved caused him to teeter for a while at the edge of insanity. He lost his job because he stopped going to work; let the mortgage payments pile up because he was flat broke, and eventually lost his house too. That's how come he ended up in his grandma's house that looks utterly decrepit now since he's failed to keep up with the maintenance of it. Charlie fell on hard luck over ten years ago and never caught himself, despite how many times a couple of the sisters counselled him and always helped him. He's a sad case."

"Yes. That's sad indeed." Joe sighed. "You call him *Old* Charlie, yet Mother referred to him as healthy and strapping. How old is this man?"

"He's actually in his early sixties," she replied. "Everyone around the neighborhood calls him Old Charlie. Who knows? — That name might've latched on to him from he was young."

"I see. So, what happened after Mother Elizabeth spoke to him that way?"

"Well, he cursed her out and never came back. Apparently, Sister Angelica and Sister Rosa have stopped by his place a few times and dropped off some food items to him without Mother's knowledge. So, he's still being looked after," she explained.

"Very good."

"The fact of the matter is that Mother Elizabeth has managed to offend practically all of us in here and countless others out there, so anyone—near or far—would likely make a good suspect in my book."

"I'm afraid you might be right. Tell me, Sister…who was it that informed the police that Mike had threatened Mother Elizabeth the day of the argument?"

"I have no idea. Someone said Mike threatened her life?"

"Yes, and unfortunately, the police are withholding that person's identity—for now, anyway."

"I haven't heard of a threat," Gertrude said. "Sister Abigail Fairchild was outside picking flowers for the vase when the incident occurred. She had a front row seat to the entire spectacle, although some of the rest of us caught at least a portion of it. Would you like for me to call her in here?"

"That would be great, thanks."

She picked up the phone.

"Where is Sister Abigail?" She asked Claire Hans. "Please go find her and ask her to come to the office right away."

Gertrude hung up, looked at Joe and said in a lowered voice, "Have you heard that the police came and questioned all of us again— privately this time—the day after the murder?"

Joe leaned forward slightly. "No. I didn't know that."

"Oh! Yes indeed. They just showed up too, probably wanting to catch us off guard. Only God knows what any of the sisters might've said, and very few spoke about their interview after they left the room. At least, I hadn't heard much of anything. Angelica told me they were trying to get her to name whom she thought might've been the most probable suspect. They tried the same thing with me, but I gave them nothing because I had nothing concrete to offer. I felt if they wanted suspects, they should go out there and find them instead of looking for an easy way out."

"I agree."

"Look at how quickly they made an arrest! I don't believe there was any real investigation conducted."

"My sentiments exactly," Joe said. "It's like someone just handed them a suspect on a silver platter and the quicker this thing goes away, the better it would be for the powers that be."

There was a light knock at the door and Abigail Fairchild walked in.

"Good morning, Father," she said.

"Good morning, Sister," Joe replied, on turning.

Abigail looked at Gertrude. "You wanted to see me, Sister?"

"Yes, please come in and shut the door."

Gertrude was obviously already operating in the new role she anticipated.

Abigail proceeded to take a seat next to Joe.

Having seen Abigail enter the room, Sisters Hannah Bowleg and Marianne Petersen approached the door and pressed their ears up against it.

"What are they talking about in there?" Marianne whispered to Hannah.

Hannah arched her brow. "Must be serious."

Gertrude turned to Abigail. "Father Joe McCullen has a question I thought you might be able to answer," she said.

Abigail looked at him.

"Yes, Sister. I understand that you were nearby when Mother Elizabeth and Mike Tenney had an issue about the lawn care last week?" he said.

"Yes. I was outside picking flowers when I heard Mother arguing with him," she replied.

"What exactly did you hear?"

Abigail glanced at Gertrude, the said, "Mother was highly upset because Mike hadn't trimmed the shrubs much to her liking. She went on about how he was lazy and had it too easy."

"What did Mike say?" Joe asked.

"Mike told her he clipped the shrubs exactly the same way he did last month when we needed him and she didn't have any qualms about it then. Said he took most of the branches and leaves off. But Mother contended that it was a lousy job and the shrubs were not clipped properly. She demanded that he get it right—in so many words. Mike said he'd go back and clip them some more, but that didn't seem to satisfy her."

Joe and Gertrude listened intently.

"She called him names; said that you, Father Joe, had spoiled him or something to that effect, and that she was going to have a word with you. Mike went and quickly clipped the shrubs some more and after that, he left on his bicycle."

"So, you were out there for a good while?" Joe said.

"Pretty much. To be honest, I could've finished with the flowers a bit earlier, but I'm ashamed to admit that I was being a little nosy."

"Sister Abigail …did you hear Mike say anything else to Mother Elizabeth—like threaten her in any way?" he asked.

Abigail grimaced. "Threatened her? Goodness—*No!* He barely answered her back—only what I told you."

"Are you sure?" Gertrude probed.

"Yes, I'm sure." She glanced at both of them. "Did someone say that Mike did that?"

Gertrude nodded. "Apparently so."

"But…that's not true. I heard the entire conversation. Who would've said that?"

"We don't know. That's what we're trying to find out."

* * * *

"Sisters, are you eavesdropping?" Angelica whispered loudly to Marianne and

Hannah whose ears had been glued outside the wooden door. "Get away from that door and back to your chores!"

The nuns apologized and hurried off in the direction of the kitchen.

Angelica sighed heavily and continued down the hallway.

* * * *

"Was there anyone else outside that you noticed when this incident occurred?" Joe asked Abigail.

"There were a few passersby. People around the neighborhood were just going about their business," she replied.

Joe nodded, and a few moments of silence ensued.

"Is that all, Father?" Gertrude asked.

"Yes. Thank you, Sister Abigail." He smiled.

"You're welcome, Father."

Gertrude thanked her as well and gestured for her to leave.

Abigail got up and headed for the door.

"You don't need to close it," Gertrude told her.

"Yes, Sister."

She left the room.

"Was that helpful in any way?" Gertrude asked Joe.

"Tremendously," he said. "Her account of that incident certainly created more questions than answers, but it established one thing…"

"And that is…"

"That I was right in my suspicion that someone *somewhere* is trying to frame Mike for Mother Elizabeth's murder. If we can find out who called the police about that bogus threat we'd be closer to solving this mystery. There's no way that Mike is going to jail and have his life ruined over a false accusation. Over my dead body!"

"I must agree that the entire investigation is very fishy. I'm not sure that I trust Wally Profado heading it; he doesn't have the best reputation in our diocese. That Kenna woman seems more trustworthy to me, but I really don't know."

She paused for a second. "What I can do is speak with the sisters individually and find out if any of them had informed the police about this supposed threat. That is, unless you'd like to question them yourself. However, I must tell you that if we have a bad seed in this bunch, we can hardly expect that person to be truthful with either of us."

"I appreciate the offer, but I would like to be present for such an undertaking."

"I completely understand! Should I call them for a brief meeting now or would another time suit your schedule?"

"If we can get it done now while I'm here, that would be perfect," he replied.

"Just wait here." Gertrude got up and walked out of the room.

Minutes later, she returned with her fellow sisters—all except Abigail.

Joe and the nuns exchanged pleasantries.

"I assembled all of you here because Father Joe is attempting to get to the bottom of what has happened to Mother Elizabeth—and to Mike Tenney—whom you all should know by now has been arrested for her murder."

The nuns were standing quietly. Angelica and Sarah were nearest to the door and Marianne and Hannah were standing together a few feet away from her. Anna was near the front.

"Mike Tenney is also one of our own and I tend to believe, along with Father Joe, that this young man is innocent of this crime and has been wrongly implicated by someone. I would like to ask if any of you present have told the police that you overheard Mike threaten Mother Elizabeth's life when she reprimanded him on the grounds of the convent last week."

There was muttering amongst them and each of them said, *No*.

"So, no one here has said any such thing to the police?" Gertrude reiterated.

They were all shaking their heads. Claire, Ruth, Pleasant and the others seemed baffled and Joe was looking around the room, hoping to read their expressions.

Gertrude looked at Father Joe and shrugged. "Well, there you have it."

Joe stood up. "Thank you, Sisters. Your honesty is greatly appreciated."

"You may leave now," Gertrude told the nuns who quickly vacated the room.

Gertrude sauntered over to Joe.

"If one of the sisters told the police that Mike threatened Mother Elizabeth last week and it wasn't true…" she started.

"Then we likely have found our killer."

"Like I said…the truth isn't guaranteed if there's a bad seed in the bunch. However, I assure you that if there is, I will be the one to weed it out. It may not be today or even tomorrow…but it will happen."

"Thank you for everything, Sister. You have been most helpful," Joe replied.

"Allow me to see you out."

They walked together toward the front door.

"When will you all be returning to the convent?" Joe asked her.

"Next week, in fact! We got the go ahead to do so a couple of days ago, but we weren't quite ready yet. Wanted to give it a little more time."

"I see. Well, have a good day, Sister," he said.

"You too, Father. And I will keep young Mike in my prayers."

"Please do."

He walked off and headed for his car.

* * * *

Joe was in his study reading a newspaper article when the doorbell rang. He folded the paper in half and went to the door.

"Morning, Father," Jim Cruz walked in, somberly.

"Father..." Sue followed with her head hung low.

Joe looked at them curiously. "What happened at the arraignment?"

They all stood near the door.

"Did they grant him bail?" Joe asked.

"I'm afraid not," Jim said. "The judge refused based on the severity of the crime."

Deeply disappointed, Joe took a seat on the sofa. Sue and Jim sat down as well.

The silence in the room felt like an eternity as Joe contemplated how difficult it must be for Mike being detained in a strange place for at least months before his trial date.

Just then, the door creaked open and Joe turned in that direction.

"Hi, Father..." Mike stood in the doorway.

Joe smiled and looked at the guilty pair, then he went to greet the boy.

The two embraced warmly and Sue was smiling from ear to ear.

"Fooled ya!" Mike said.

"I'm glad Sunday is just two days away," Joe remarked as they walked over to the living room.

"Why's that?" Jim asked.

"Because I know the three of you will be at Mass. God knows you need it."

They all laughed heartily.

"So, how are you, Mike? What was it like at the juvenile facility?" Joe asked.

Mike was sitting next to his mother. "Weird. Being around the other kids didn't bother me. It was just being there knowing I shouldn't be that was hard. But I guess it still beats the big house."

"You got that right!" Joe replied. "Anything beats that. If you were eighteen, that's where they would've put you. Do you know that?"

"Nope."

"Father's right," Jim said. "You would've been right there with the hardened criminals."

"God is merciful…" Sue rubbed her son's back. "I'm so glad you'll be coming back home with me. I didn't sleep a wink last night."

Mike held his mother close.

"So, tell me about it, Jim—the arraignment." Joe sat back comfortably.

"Well, I put forward a strong case for Mike being granted bail and the judge bought it," he said.

"Awesome." Joe smiled.

"You noticed he's not wearing any ankle monitor either, right?"

Joe glanced at the boy's legs. "Hadn't thought about that. How'd you pull that off?"

"Easy—I presented a good character reference, which happened to be my own. I gave a concise background of Mike having been raised in the church, placed under your wing for guidance and how I would personally take responsibility for him showing up to court when the time comes. I reminded the judge that the boy is innocent until proven guilty."

"That prosecutor woman fought tooth and nail to keep Mike detained though," Sue chimed in.

Mike was nodding.

"Yep," Jim agreed, "but that's why it was me sitting there with Mike and not another attorney. I'm good at what I do—if I do say so myself."

"Be bright and early to Mass, Jim," Joe said.

Jim chuckled. "Anyway, the trial is set for six months from now, so that gives us enough time…"

"To find out who the real killer is," Joe interjected.

8

Sue watched proudly from the pew as Mike performed his duties as altar boy that Sunday morning. Her heart bursting with gratitude, she used her handkerchief to dry the tears that had slid down her cheeks. Yet, as emotional as the moment was for her, she was also aware of the whispers and the snickering behind her back— but she didn't care. Mike was with her again and for now, it was all that mattered.

Wally Profado and his wife were seated on the fourth pew from the front. Sue glanced over at them and quickly chased the thought that had crossed her mind. She would've felt guilty if she'd allowed herself to dwell on it, especially in the sanctuary.

"Lovely service, Father." April Johnson shook Joe's hand after Mass. She was with her husband Matt whose facial expression depicted that he'd been dragged to church and possibly held at gunpoint.

"Thank you, April." Joe said. "Matt, nice seeing you again this Sunday."

Matt forced a smile. "Well, we'll be going, Father. Enjoy your Sunday dinner."

"I will."

Joe shook the hands of a few other parishioners filing out of the church before Sandra Metstrom showed up.

"Father, may I have a word…privately?" she asked.

"Sure." Joe stepped aside several feet away from the crowd.

Sandra, a spinster, was in her early sixties and lived alone. She was a recently retired general manager of the town's water company—a position she'd held for twenty years.

"I don't mean to come across the wrong way, Father." she started. "But I don't believe I would be out of line in saying what it is I have to say since I, my parents and other Metstroms have generously supported this parish for many years even before you were transferred here."

"Okay…" Joe waited.

"That boy—Mike Tenney has been accused of slaughtering our beloved Mother Elizabeth Rhinehart. And to say that I was shocked to see him here at church and moreover, still serving as an altar boy, is an understatement. It nearly sent me into hysterics on my pew!"

"Really?" Joe grimaced. "We certainly wouldn't want that."

"Why in the world would you allow him to move about this sanctuary as if nothing has happened—as if he isn't a coldblooded murderer?"

"Let me ask you a question, Sandra…"

"Yes?" She slid the strap of her pink purse further up her forearm.

"If your brother Harold had been accused of such a crime and there was no concrete proof that he was actually guilty of it, despite his profession of innocence, would you appreciate this church shunning him?" Joe asked.

She hesitated for a moment, then said, "Mike Tenney was arrested for the crime, Father!"

"But he is innocent until proven guilty. No court convicted that young man of anything.

So, as far as I am concerned—and the archbishop fully agrees—he is not to be treated like a convicted criminal; he is a member of this church just as you are. And may I remind you of what our Lord taught us, which is that we ought to treat others in the manner we wish to be treated. Now, if there's nothing further…"

Sandra yanked her purse from her arm, gripping it tightly in her hand, and abruptly walked off. Her behavior undoubtedly turned a few heads.

Joe politely joined the other parishioners still filing out of the church.

"Is everything all right, Father?" Luke Bosfield, a middle-aged marine asked as he shook Joe's hand. He was with his wife Belinda who was holding their infant daughter.

"I'm splendid, Luke! Good to see you all, especially this little cutie of yours!"

He gently touched the child's fingers. "She's absolutely adorable."

"Thank you, Father." Belinda smiled. "Wonderful homily, as always."

"Thank you, dear. Y'all take care and be safe."

"You too," Luke answered as they were leaving.

Being the last ones there, Sue and Mike waited outside as Joe secured the front door.

"Is everything all right?" He looked at them, keys dangling in his hand.

"Everything's good," Mike said.

Sue turned to him. "You sure?"

"Yeah. If you're wondering if anyone showed me any *funniness*, I'd have to say *no*—at least for the most part. Everybody acted like nothing happened; I really don't think they believe I did it. Only Rob seemed a bit standoffish, but I don't care. Not everyone is gonna believe in you."

"You said it," Joe replied. "And what you need to remember is that you don't need anyone's approval. People will have their theories no matter what you say or do. Live life, be yourself and trust God to vindicate you. That's all."

Sue was nodding in agreement.

"I wouldn't stand here and pretend like it's gonna be easy until this is all cleared up." He gripped his shoulder. "You will have your challenges, Mike, but you've got all the support you need, okay?"

"Okay," Mike replied.

"Now y'all go home, have dinner and relax because that's exactly what I'm about to do."

Joe happily headed for the rectory where his chef had his favorite Sunday dish prepared.

* * * *

"Mom! You missed the turn!" Mike exclaimed.

Sue slowed her car slightly and glanced through the rearview mirror. "I don't know where my mind was," she said, making a U-turn.

Mike studied her closely. "Are you all right, Mom?"

"Sure, I am!" She smiled. "Why do you ask?"

"Because you seem preoccupied."

She patted his leg. "I'm fine—really. Just so grateful that you're out of that juvenile hall."

He looked blankly to his right. "You're worried. Aren't you?"

"Worried? Have you forgotten who's on the case? None other than Jim Cruz and the best investigators this li'l town has ever seen. Before you know it, this whole mess'll be a thing of the past."

He looked her way again and could see the worry on her face. Sue was never good at hiding her feelings.

"You can't fool me, Mom. I know you're still scared about all the possibilities, but I want you to know that whatever happens, I'll be fine; I'm a tough kid. You know nothing can break me."

"I know, honey. I know." She fought back the tears welling in her eyes.

"The only thing I wouldn't be able to handle is the thought that you were at home stressing over me and there's nothing I could do about it. I can't afford for you to get sick with worry, Mom. You're all I have."

She nodded quickly and with a few sniffles said, "I promise I'm fine and I also promise that we'll get through this, son. God is a vindicator."

"He is."

Sue pulled onto the carport of the little white house she'd owned for fifteen years. She was only living there for one year before she'd taken Mike in and felt proud knowing she'd saved enough on her own to come up with a down payment for it. In November, she'd be making her last mortgage payment. And looking at the house with that brief thought in mind, she wondered how a year filled with much promise and gratification could also be one filled with sadness and distress. Not wanting Mike to sense her worry, she quickly chased away the thought and switched off the engine.

"I can't wait to dig in! I'm so glad you cook dinner on Sunday mornings, instead of waiting until we get back from church." He got out of the car and headed for the front door.

"Wash up first!" she insisted as he used his keys to enter the house.

"You're eating so early, young man. You're gonna be hungry again in an hour!" Sue said after a change of clothes. Mike was in the TV room eating and enjoying a football game.

"I'm glad you cooked enough for me to get seconds." He smiled, biting into his fried chicken wing.

"When you're done, the garbage needs to go out. It's filled to the brim."

"I'll take care of it."

Sue retired to her bedroom. She always took a half hour to hour's nap after Mass and often ate dinner later in the afternoon. She'd just started to doze off when she heard a crashing sound outside and a vehicle skidding off.

Mike was already outside when she ran out of the bedroom. He was standing on their driveway looking at the wall.

"What was that?" Sue frowned.

She turned in the direction of his stare. "My God! What in the hell…?"

In large, black lettering on the front wall of their house were the words: *Cold blooded murderer!* She also noticed the knocked over trash can near the carport.

"How can anyone do this? The nerve of these people!" Sue was furious.

"I'll paint over it, Mom. Don't worry about those jerks," Mike said.

"We should call the police."

"For what? Because someone sprayed graffiti on our wall and knocked over our trash can? They're not gonna go looking for them; you'd just be wasting your time. Besides, they might be glad those idiots did this to us."

"It's just so unfair!" she yelled. "I swear, if I had a gun and had caught them in the act, I'd have shot them dead on the spot."

"No, you wouldn't have!" Mike exclaimed. "And where do you get off swearing, Mom? You just hollered at me for doing the same thing the other day."

She was shaking her head in frustration.

"Don't let this upset you," he said. It's probably just a couple of punk kids getting into mischief. They're not worth the headache."

Her face softened as she saw the maturity in his eyes. She was supposed to be the one assuring him."

"You sound like Father Joe," she said.

"I wonder if that's a good thing."

For added security, Mike locked the front gate and let their Doberman Pinscher out of the back fence to freely roam the yard. Mike reopened a gallon of paint that had been stored since the house was retouched the previous Christmas and painted over the graffiti. With anger brewing on the inside, he recalled what Father Joe had said after Mass that day. Despite what he'd told his mother, he wished he knew who was bold enough to enter their property and deface their home.

And he wished he could make them pay.

9

*C*couple of hours after enjoying his Sunday dinner, Joe was walking alone on the quiet convent grounds dotted with mid-sized and tall trees; their flowers in full bloom. He even saw a bird's nest in one of them and what he presumed was the mother bird on a nearby branch. He thought of how even birds knew how to nurture and protect their young and he smiled.

He stopped for a few moments and looked around at the large property with two supreme white structures on it. The place had a peaceful air about it despite its tranquility being shattered by the murder of one of its own. The yellow barricade tape was all gone; only a few shreds of it could be spotted here and there. Joe certainly understood the nuns' reluctance to return so soon.

He resumed his walk, now looking more closely at the convent itself—the doors and windows, in particular. He was hoping to find something somewhere that might reveal the killer's true point of entry since that fact was clearly unknown.

Could it be as Gertrude suspects? he wondered. *Could a nun really have done the unthinkable?* He shuddered at the thought which almost made him sick to his stomach. *Could evil have really penetrated such a place?*

He sighed deeply, suddenly feeling the weight of the world on his shoulders.

"Lord, help me to find the truth," he muttered, looking to the heavens.

"Father!" He heard someone call a distance off. Turning abruptly toward the sidewalk, he saw a man waving, so he waved back. "Hey there! How are you today?"

"I'm fine. Horrible thing that happened here!" the stranger said.

Joe hurried over to him.

"Yes, yes. It's a terrible tragedy indeed." He was nearly out of breath when he arrived.

The man appeared to be in his thirties. Ruffled hair, scrawny, unshaven and Joe noticed that his body odor wasn't the best either.

"Heard a nun got killed. Who in the world would wanna do that?" he said.

"Same thing I'm wondering," Joe replied. "Do you live in the neighborhood?"

"Right around the block there on Garner Street. I take care of my elderly mother; have been for the past year."

"You're a good son."

"Not really, Father," he responded, looking a bit dismayed. "I haven't always been this way. I put my mother through hell for years when I struggled with a meth addiction. Cleaned myself up after she got sick, and I found out it's terminal. She has cancer."

"I'm very sorry to hear that, son. Would you like for me to pay her a visit and pray with her?"

He immediately shook his head. "I appreciate your offer, but Mom isn't religious—never has been, and she wouldn't take too kindly to me bringin' a preacher in her house." He grinned.

"Well, there's no distance in prayer; I will still pray for her. What's her name?"

"Betty… Betty Cook."

"I'll be sure to send up a prayer on her behalf," Joe said.

"I'm Peter Callaghan…by the way." He extended his hand.

"Nice to meet you, Peter. I'm Father Joe McCullen. I'd like to invite you to Mass."

He told him the address and service times.

"Actually, here's my card." Joe conveniently slid one out of his wallet. "Both the church number and my cell are on there."

Peter gazed down at the card. "Thank you, Father. Will think about the church thing; nice of you to offer."

"Would be happy to have you. We're not big on dressing up fancy or anything, so come as you are. No pressure."

Peter nodded, gratefully.

"I saw someone here that night, you know," he revealed, much to Joe's surprise. "Looks like he was sneakin' around."

"You mean…"

"The night that head nun got killed."

Joe was intrigued. "Who did you see?"

"Well, I don't know the guy! But I could see him clear as day because of all the lampposts lightenin' up the property," he replied. "He was short, a little stocky, had blonde hair—I'm sure of it. I wondered what he was doing, but at the same time, I wasn't about to ask. I had a sick mother at home to get to and I'd already overstayed my time slammin' dominoes with a couple buddies of mine."

Joe got out his cell phone this time and pulled up Mike Tenney's Facebook page. "From what you said, he doesn't seem to fit the description, but would this happen to be the guy you saw?"

Peter leaned in and immediately shook his head. "That's not him! I told you the guy I saw was short and stocky. That guy's tall and pretty well built," he said.

"I just wanted to make sure."

"Who is this guy?"

"He's the one they've charged for Mother Elizabeth's murder, I'm afraid."

Peter arched his brows. "Well, I don't know if they've got the right guy or not. I only know I saw someone sneakin' around this property. I have no idea if he killed anyone."

"Yes. That's true," Joe replied. "Tell me, Peter…have you told the police what you saw that night?"

"Told the police? I ain't goin' within three yards of a police station to tell them nothin' they ain't asked me. I had enough run ins with them already when I used to be strung out. Now, if they come find me, I'll voluntarily tell them what I saw, but if they ain't askin', I ain't tellin'."

"Would you mind if I told an acquaintance of mine who happens to be a private investigator working the case to follow up with you and you tell him what you saw?" Joe asked.

Peter thought for a moment. "Let me ask you something, Father. Is that young fella you showed me a good guy?" he asked.

"Yes. He's like a son to me," Joe replied. "I know he's innocent."

"Well, since you seem like a good guy yourself, and you have that kind of faith in him, I'd be willin' to tell your PI or even the cops what I saw."

Joe breathed a sigh of relief.

"You can tell them I live right there on Garner Street, second house on the right after you turn through the corner. It's green, trimmed white, number thirty."

Joe quickly typed the info in the notes section of his cell phone.

"Thank you, Peter. You're a great man—and you have a great name too."

"Like Peter in the Bible." He smiled.

"Right."

As he drove away from the convent that day, Joe decided not to share what he learned with Sue and Mike until he knew more. That way, they wouldn't be disappointed if the lead went nowhere.

10

S andra Metstrom and seven other women were at the archbishop's office bright and early Monday morning. After confirming that His Excellency would see them, Joan Armstrong, his secretary, led them to the conference room where they patiently waited. Sandra was instrumental in rounding up some of the ladies active in the women's ministry at church—all between the ages of forty-eight and seventy-five. Diana Coffey being the youngest and Maxine Dunbar, the eldest. Maxine, along with Sandra came from a wealthy and influential line of business owners, politicians and attorneys most of which made the church their second home and were active there in some regard.

Archbishop Simms entered the office ten minutes later, and as was customary, everyone stood. Joan Armstrong followed with a legal notepad and a pen in hand.

"Good morning, everyone," Simms said.

"Good morning, Your Excellency," the women replied.

After Simms had taken his seat, Joan joined them at the table and sat at the far end, prepared to record the minutes.

The meeting commenced with a brief prayer, then Simms looked at the group and asked, "What can I do for you ladies today?"

Sandra leaned forward. "Your Excellency, we, the members of the women's ministry of our parish decided to pay a visit to you with regards to Mike Tenney, the young man as you know, who was accused of slaughtering Mother Elizabeth Rhinehart," she said.

"Slaughtering?" He grimaced.

"Yes."

"Go on."

"Well, he was at Mass yesterday participating in altar duties and acting as if nothing happened. Being a faithful member of our parish, after service I went and complained about that to Father Joe McCullen and I literally got a brush off, to put it bluntly!"

Simms quietly listened.

"So, when I got home, I phoned some members of our ministry to hear their thoughts on the matter," she continued. "And the majority agreed that the young man should *not* be allowed to participate in any duties concerning the church as long as he's a murder suspect."

Her supporters were all nodding in agreement.

Simms folded his arms and sighed. "Sandra, I appreciate your sentiments and those of all the ladies here, but I am aware of Mike Tenney's position—Father Joe and I discussed it. We both agree that he is innocent unless proven guilty, as heinous as the crime was. Personally, I don't believe the police have conducted a thorough enough investigation to arrive at the conclusion that it was this teenager who grew up in the church that committed this crime. Therefore, without any concrete proof that he is guilty, I agree with Father Joe that he should not be deprived of his altar duties at the church. And if, by chance, I have made the wrong call, this is not the setting where I will be made to answer for it."

"Well, I disagree with you!" Sandra blurted. "We all do! Don't we?" She glanced at the ladies she'd brought along.

Their mutters of support for her filled the room.

"I am sorry you all disagree, but I believe in being fair to everyone," Simms stated. "Rumors and circumstantial evidence are not enough to convince me that a member of this diocese is guilty of murder."

"It's enough for me!" Maxine said. "I have the utmost respect for you, Your Excellency, but I believe you are not seeing this picture clearly. How would we look as a church allowing someone accused of murdering one of our own to continue to serve? How would other denominations view us? We are supposed to set a good example, and being slack with such a serious issue as this is not doing that."

"I agree!" Grace Witmore, who was sitting next to her said.

"Ladies, please settle down," Joan interjected.

Sandra looked Simms directly in the eyes. "Has your position changed, Archbishop?" she asked.

"No, it hasn't. I made my position very clear," he replied.

"Well, since that's the case, we will be going above your head to request your immediate removal from this esteemed position you hold, obviously undeservedly. What you are upholding is not what the church stands for. Some of our families have generously contributed to the running of our parish and to the diocese as a whole, and your behavior is unacceptable!"

"Allow me to clear up something and I trust that once will be enough," Simms started. "Just because your family may have generously contributed to the church does not mean that you, I or any other human being *owns* the church. The church belongs to God. Whatever we do should be for His glory and edification and not our own. So, thank you for your contributions, but my position in this matter still stands."

Sandra abruptly stood up. "Good day, Your Excellency. Let's go, ladies. We have a letter to write!"

They all got up and headed for the door.

Joan looked at Simms from the other side of the desk, unsure of what to say. He only shook his head, then got up and left the room.

* * * *

"Would you believe those jerks did this to us?" Sue showed Father Joe a snapshot of the graffiti on the wall of her house taken from her cell phone. She was standing next to his chair as he signed a stack of checks.

Joe was utilizing the little room in the church office, which he seldomly ever occupied. The rectory, just fifty yards away was his habitat and place of business rolled into one.

He looked at the photo. "Someone actually sprayed this on your wall?"

"Yep."

"Cowards! They wait until you're gone to do it."

"We were at home when it happened," Sue informed him.

"Say what?" He almost looked at her cross-eyed.

Suddenly, a bit embarrassed, she nodded.

"Wait. Let me get this straight. Someone or some *people* came into your yard and sprayed graffiti on the front wall of your house while y'all were inside?"

Sue just stared, knowing what was coming next.

"You've got to be kidding!" He laughed.

"This is no laughing matter, Father. I was highly upset yesterday, and poor Mike had to go and paint over it before any of the neighbors noticed."

"You're right. It's no laughing matter. Please forgive me." He wiped the smile from his face. "But where was your dog? Dead to the world too?"

"Smokey was in the backyard. We let him out of the fence now, so I dare those jerks to come back."

"Did you call the police?" Joe asked.

She shook her head. "The culprits had already taken off. I doubt they would've found them. With Smokey having free rein, I'm sure we won't have that problem anymore."

Joe sighed. "I hope you're right."

Virginia Adams appeared at the door. "Excuse me, Father. Adele and David Smith are here to see you," she said.

Sue immediately walked out of the office, not making eye contact with Virginia as she passed by.

"Oh! Send them in," Joe answered.

"Yes, Father."

Virginia approached the couple who were waiting out front. "Father Joe will see you now."

She led them to the office, then shut the door behind them.

Joe stood up and extended his hand to each of them. "Lovely to see both of you again."

"Thank you, Father," David said.

"Please have a seat."

David allowed his wife to sit first.

"To what do I owe this pleasure today?" Joe smiled.

Adele Smith was a brunette with fair skin and narrow features. She was well put together and very poised. Her husband, on the other hand, was a jeans and T-shirt kind of guy, a little thick around the waist and had a pleasant face.

"Father, first of all, we'd like to thank you for being gracious enough to allow us and our teenage daughter Emily to take the Beginners classes together instead of us having to split up. It really saves us from having a lot of back and forth, and makes officially entering the church much easier for us."

"You're welcome." Joe nodded. "Of course, as I explained to you all weeks ago, it is not the normal procedure, but I do have the liberty to make certain decisions at my discretion. And I'm pleased to be of help to your family as you make your transition into the church."

"Well, everything was going fairly well when Mother Elizabeth was in charge of the program. She accepted us as a family and we had no qualms other than the times she was a bit *impatient*, for lack of a better word." She paused. "God rest the dead. But since Cynthia Mason took over the program after Mother Elizabeth's unfortunate passing, she's been giving all of us—David, Emily and I—the cold shoulder as if we're not supposed to be there."

"Really?" Joe frowned.

David was nodding.

"I made it a point to explain to her the arrangement we had when she first came on and she seemed to scoff at the idea, saying that it would've been better for Emily to be with her peers during the process," Adele continued. "Although she may have had a point, we all know what works better for us as a family since we live so far away from the church. She's been treating us very coldly ever since the first day she started."

"In what way?" Joe pressed.

"Well, during the meetings, she very rarely looks our way whenever she asks questions. And when any of us goes ahead and answers, she doesn't respond—almost as if we're not supposed to be included. She's just very standoffish towards us and it's become extremely uncomfortable for us. The only reason we haven't dropped out of the class is because we truly want to become members of this church and I personally don't believe that we should allow one person to stop that from happening!"

"And I agree with you wholeheartedly," Joe replied. "Look...I'm gonna be straight up with you. If that's the vibe you're getting from Cynthia, it's wrong and totally unacceptable. The service she provides for the church is of a voluntary nature and while we are grateful for such a sacrifice of one's time and energy, if that is her attitude and she doesn't perform the service the way the church requires, no one is holding a gun to her head. She's free to leave on the next train smokin', so to speak. Mistreating others and being the cause of them potentially turning away from the church before they've even gotten a foot inside the door will not be tolerated here. Rest assured, I will have a word with her and it's highly unlikely that she will be a problem anymore. But if, by chance, she is, don't hesitate to let me know and I'll deal with the matter another way."

"Thank you, Father," Adele said, rising to her feet, along with her husband. "We knew that coming here was the right decision."

"Yes, thank you so much, Father," David said. "Believe me, we wouldn't have come to you if we felt we could've just continued to cope with things the way they are."

"No! No! I'm glad you came. You're a good couple and you have a lovely family. I'm happy to help in any way I can."

As they turned to leave, Joe suddenly thought of something.

"By the way, since you both are here…did you happen to notice anything about Mother Elizabeth or anyone else's interactions with her during your meetings that might've alarmed you?" he asked.

Adele and David glanced at each other.

"There was this one time…" Adele started. "A young woman came to the door one Monday night about a half hour after our class had started and asked Mother Elizabeth if she could have a word with her outside. By the way they interacted with each other initially, it seemed like they knew one another. I was seated on the left side of the table facing the door, so I could pretty much see what was going on. Well, within a minute or so, the conversation obviously took a turn. Although they weren't speaking loudly enough for me to make out what they were saying, they were definitely arguing. Soon, the woman walked off leaving Mother there staring into the distance for a while, then she came back inside."

"Was she upset when she returned?" Joe asked.

"I'm sure that *upset* isn't the word I should use. She seemed a little bothered. It's hard to describe, but she did go on with the meeting as usual and after a while seemed okay again."

"Can you describe this woman you saw?"

"She was probably in her early twenties, thin, about five-feet-ten inches tall; had shoulder-length black hair and…"

"She had a mole on her face, right by her nose," David added.

Joe thought for a moment. The description they provided didn't ring a bell.

"Was that the only incident?" he asked them.

They glanced at each other again and Adele answered, "Yep. That's the only one that I recall. I wouldn't necessarily call it *alarming*, but it certainly caught my attention."

"Thank you," Joe replied. "Well, it was nice seeing you two again." He led the way to the door. "How's Emily, doing?"

"She's great!" David said.

"Studying hard to finish high school strong?" Joe asked.

"Yes, sir. She's a studious young girl. Taking extra SAT classes after school to hopefully, get great scores and land a scholarship when she graduates," the proud dad replied.

"What does she want to do?"

"She wants to be a cardiologist," Adele promptly interjected. "She got her inspiration when her grandfather, David's dad was in hospital a few years ago with heart problems."

"I see. Did your Father recover?" he asked David.

"Yes, he's doing well. On a lot of meds, but we're thankful he's still here."

"He's blessed, for sure." Joe stepped aside at the door. "Y'all take care and be safe out there on the road."

"Thank you, Father. We will," David replied.

After they left, Joe retrieved the signed checks from his desk and closed the door behind him.

"All done." He handed the checks to Virginia who was sitting at her desk.

"Is everything all right with the Smiths, Father," she asked, resting the checks in front of her.

"Yes, they're fine. It's nothing I can't handle," he replied before heading to the door.

* * * *

On Monday evenings, Cynthia Mason usually arrived at church an hour prior to the start of her six o'clock Beginners class. She was six feet tall, lean and a stickler for promptness. Cynthia was married, but to an absent husband. Steve Mason had run off fourteen years earlier to be with his mistress, whom he claimed was the true love of his life. Not without telling her and the children that Cynthia was impossible to live with and he'd rather co-exist under a bridge with a pig than to spend one more second with Cynthia. By all accounts, Mrs. Mason was domineering and had ruled her house with an iron fist which is the reason her two children Steve Jr. and Lenora also moved out the minute they hit eighteen. Junior readily enrolled in the army and Lenora moved in with her boyfriend despite her mother's protests. Cynthia was all alone in that big house of hers.

She'd made her millions as a stockbroker and was able to comfortably retire at age forty. Steve had kept his job as a store manager, refusing to depend solely upon his wife's money, and the thought of spending more hours in the day with her than he had to terrified him.

"Cynthia, Father Joe has asked to see you," Tina Delong told her at the door of the meeting room. Cynthia was at the desk organizing articles she'd copied for that night's class.

"At the rectory?" Cynthia asked.

"No. He's inside the church."

Tina walked off.

Cynthia slid back her chair and headed for the sanctuary.

Inside, members of the choir were beginning to assemble in the eastern corner near the instruments to commence their practice for the following Sunday. Cynthia spotted Joe sitting alone in the front pew on the right.

"Good evening, Father," she said. "You asked to see me?"

"Good evening, Cynthia," Joe replied, resting his cell phone aside. "Please come and sit with me for a minute."

She walked over and sat down next to him.

"First off, I want to thank you for stepping up to the plate and offering to take over the Beginners classes after the unfortunate passing of Mother Elizabeth."

"It's the least I could do to help out," she replied.

"How is it going so far?"

"Fine. Thank you," she said. "What is this about, if you don't mind me getting straight to the point?"

"The Smith family. How are things working out with them?"

"I suppose, the same way it's working out for everyone else, Father."

He shifted to a more comfortable position. "Are you uncomfortable with the arrangement I put in place regarding the family?" he asked.

"Well—I'm not in favor of it, to be perfectly honest. Other families must go through the normal process the church had put in place for obvious reasons, while this family gets to bypass it. Why are they more important than other people?"

Joe was not surprised by her bluntness, neither by the jealousy she couldn't possibly conceal.

"The Smiths are not more important than other people, as you say," he replied. "They do, however, find themselves in a situation where splitting up the classes would put them at a major disadvantage. As rector of this parish, I sought a way to ease the burden for the family as it relates to that, which is in my capacity to do, as you are aware. With that said, the reason I have asked to see you was to let you know that the Smiths have expressed that they are very ill at ease with the way you are allegedly treating them because of the said arrangement. They feel a sort of *coldness* when they're in your presence."

"They said that?"

Joe only looked at her.

"How dare they? Who do they think they are coming to this church and complaining about me? I treat them the way I treat everyone else. They're not special!"

"Cynthia…Cynthia…Cynthia. Oh, how I tolerate you sometimes…"

"You what?"

"I invited you into the sanctuary instead of speaking with you elsewhere with the hopes that being here might awaken some charity within you."

Cynthia was giving him a death stare.

"The point is that while you are voluntarily serving in the capacity of program leader, the church expects you not to mistreat, agonize, antagonize, or chase away anyone the good Lord is leading to His church. If you are to continue in that service, your treatment of our brothers and sisters needs to improve. You are in a vital position. And if by chance, you do not feel that you are willing or able to adjust your behavior, don't hesitate to inform me so that we can promptly find a replacement."

Cynthia was at a loss for words.

"Please feel free to let me know, Cynthia." Joe reiterated. He glanced at his wristwatch. "Oh! It's already a quarter to six. How time flies! Don't let me keep you from your meeting."

"Good evening, Father."

She got up and left.

_____

11

Tuesday morning…

Gertrude was sitting near a window of the diner just down the street from Ructus Hill when Joe walked inside. She waved to him and he immediately hurried over to her.

"How are you today, Sister?" He sat down at the table with her.

"Grateful for another day," she said. "How are you doing, Father?"

"Better than I was two days ago."

"You said you have some information?" She asked, quietly.

A waitress appeared at the table. "Good morning, sir. Can I get you something?" she asked.

"Good morning, young lady. All is well?" he replied.

"Yes, Father."

He turned to Gertrude. "Would you like something, Sister?"

"No, I'm fine. I've still got a half a cup of coffee sitting here," she replied.

"Well, then. I'll just have a cup of coffee myself." He smiled at the waitress.

"Sugar and cream?"

"Lots of sugar and cream please," he stressed.

As the waitress walked off, Gertrude gave him a reprimanding look. "That sugar's gonna kill you, Father. You need to pay better attention to your health. You've only got one body, you know."

"I know." He agreed. "The problem is I've always had a sweet tooth. Nevertheless, you're right—I've got to do better."

She didn't respond.

"This past Sunday, I spoke with a young man who lives near the convent and we had an interesting conversation," he said.

He had her full attention. "Yes…?"

"He mentioned having seen a man lurking around the building the night before Mother Elizabeth's body was found."

"Really? Did he inform the police?"

Joe shook his head. "He was of the mentality that if you don't ask, there's nothing for him to tell."

Gertrude rolled her eyes.

"But he's agreed that if an investigator pays him a visit and asks some questions, he'll reveal what he knows," Joe explained.

"Did he tell you anything more?" she asked.

"He provided a description of the person he saw."

Her curiosity was piqued.

"Tell me…do you remember seeing a guy that match these features anywhere in the vicinity of the convent? Rather short, stocky, had blonde hair?

Gertrude thought for a second. "Kinda sounds like Henry Sears. That boy who came by our bookstore a few times." She leaned forward and spoke even more quietly. "I'm pretty sure he came by when he did—not because he was interested in books—but instead, he used it as an opportunity to see his sister Maggie who worked in the store at the time. She was with us for a short time—an aspirant. I'm sure they knew separation from family members for a while was a requirement of her being there."

"Whatever happened to Maggie?" Joe asked.

"No one really knows. One day, she just upped and left, and Mother Elizabeth was strangely tight-lipped about it."

"Did Mother have any issues with her?"

Gertrude pursed her lips and leaned back again. "Mother had issues with everyone, Father. She criticized that girl just like she did everybody else. Maggie Sears wasn't anything special," she said.

Suddenly, she looked at him suspiciously. "Do you think her brother was the one the passerby spotted at the convent that night?"

Joe retrieved his phone from his pocket and started fiddling with it. "Now that I have a name, maybe I can find a picture of him on Facebook or some other social media sight," he said without directly answering her question.

"And do what with?" Gertrude asked.

The waitress returned with a hot cup of coffee which she rested on the table in front of him.

"Thanks so much," Joe told her.

"My pleasure, Father. Enjoy."

She then walked off to another table.

Joe took a sip of his coffee and looked at Gertrude. "If I find this Henry and you identify him as Maggie's brother, I can go to Peter—the passerby—and find out if that's the guy he saw."

"Smart thinking…" She nodded. "Then Henry will have to explain to the police why he was sneaking around the convent that night."

Joe typed in *Henry Sears* in the Facebook search bar and quite a number of profiles popped up. He handed Gertrude his phone to skim through them one by one.

"That's him!" She showed him. "That's Henry—Maggie's brother.

Joe looked at the profile picture and read the information directly underneath. "He lives right here in Old Providence," he noted. "Is into textiles for a living."

"If he was at the convent that night, I wanna know why." Gertrude said.

"So do I."

He took another sip of his coffee.

                    * * * *

"That's definitely the guy I saw!" Peter exclaimed as he viewed the picture on Joe's cell phone.

The house on Garner Street was easy for Joe to find. Peter had been working on an old car when he pulled up in front of the house.

"Are you absolutely sure this is him?" Joe asked.

"Damn sure's more like it!"

Peter quickly caught himself. "Oh! Sorry, Father. That was just a slip of the tongue."

"You've been a great help to me, Peter," Joe told him, putting his phone away. He then looked towards the front door of the house that had smudgy fingerprints on the frame, mainly near the door handle. "Are you sure you don't want me to pay your mother a visit?" he asked.

"Ooh! No! No! No!" Peter whispered loudly.

Joe was taken aback by his strong aversion to it.

"Have you ever seen *The Exorcist*, Father?"

"I'm afraid I have."

"Well, I've got one thing to say… If this isn't a good day for you to see my mom's head spinning all the way 'round like that girl did in that movie, you'd better move on. Because if you step inside our house, all them demons mom's been fighting for decades gonna come out full force and then you'll have a hell of a hubble on your hands!"

"I thought you said she was terminally ill," Joe said.

Peter looked at him as if he was stupid. "Does sickness ever stop them strong demons from doing their thing, Father?"

"I suppose not."

"Well, there you have it!"

Before he left, Joe handed Peter a few dollars to help with expenses around the house although he hadn't asked him for a penny. Peter was more than grateful for the kind and timely gesture.

After getting in his car, Joe made a phone call to the archbishop and his secretary put him through right away.

"Your Excellency, I need to speak with you with regards to a former aspirant by the name of Maggie Sears…" Joe started. "Are you familiar with that name?"

The archbishop's heart sank at the very mention of it. "I am," he replied.

Following a two-minute conversation with his superior, Joe immediately made a second call.

"Jim, it's me. I have a lead," he said. "Have your PI locate the address for one Henry Sears. I'm sending you his picture now."

"Sure. Who is this guy?" Jim asked. "And what does he have to do with the case?"

"I'll explain later, as soon as I find out more. Get your guy on this right away for me please."

Jim readily obliged.

12

*L*ora Garcia drove her white hatchback into the church parking lot shortly after 4:00 P.M. She was a longstanding member of the fundraising committee and was late for their meeting that afternoon. April Garcia, seated in the front next to her mother, spotted Mike in the garden near the rectory.

"Isn't that Mike Tenney?" Lora asked after putting the car in park.

"Yes," April replied.

"To think that a boy so young would get himself arrested for murder…"

April immediately looked at her mother. "It sounds like you're judging him, Mom. Doesn't the Bible talk about us not judging others? Suppose he's innocent?"

Lora felt a sense of guilt creep on. She'd always taught her daughter to be fair and to give others the benefit of the doubt.

"You're right." She unfastened her seatbelt, then looked up towards the second floor of the office building where the meeting was being held. "Anyway, I'm already late so we'd better go. The meeting shouldn't last for more than an hour."

"Go ahead," April told her mother while getting out of the car.

Lora got out and noticed the direction where her daughter was headed.

"Where are you going?" she cried.

April kept walking and by that time, Mike had stood up in the garden, watching as she approached him.

Lora looked on from the car for a few moments.

"Hi, Mike," April said.

"Hi." He shoved his gloved hands partway into his pockets.

"How are you?"

Mike always found himself unusually shy whenever April was in his presence. Whenever she showed up, it appeared that his massive self-confidence had disintegrated to almost nothing. She was sixteen, beautiful, a straight A student, and seemingly had the perfect life and the perfect family. On occasion they chatted, but never for long.

"I'm doing okay," he said.

She looked at the garden. "What are you planting?"

He smiled. "Father said these daisies would match the color of the rectory."

"He's right," April answered, stooping over to sniff one of the flowers. "They smell nice too."

"Yeah, they do."

There was a brief pause.

Reluctantly, Lora walked off and headed up the stairs above the office.

"So, what are you doing here?" Mike asked April.

She glanced back at the room above the office. "Mom has one of those meetings. I usually sit in whenever I don't have anything else to do, but I'm not feeling that right now."

"I see."

"Can I help you plant some flowers?"

Mike grimaced. "You want to? This can be grimy work, you know."

"Doesn't matter," she said. "Do you have an extra pair of gloves? If not, I'll just use my bare hands."

"Sure! Sure, I do. I'll grab a pair from inside."

He started to leave.

"Mike wait!"

He turned and looked at her.

"For what it's worth…I just wanted to tell you that I believe you're innocent and I support you," she said.

He saw the look of sincerity in her eyes and at that moment, admired her even more. "Thank you," he replied. "It means a lot to me."

She sighed. "Okay. What are you waiting for? Go get the gloves!"

He grinned. "Sure. No problem."

Mike hurried inside the rectory.

Shortly thereafter, he returned with a pair of blue gloves and as he was about to hand them to her, he saw Wally Profado exiting his car, then walking in their direction.

"What's the matter?" April noticed the excitement had disappeared from Mike's face.

She followed his stare.

"Good morning, kids," Wally said to them, moments later.

"Good morning," they both replied. Mike's response was more of a murmur.

"Mike…" Wally stood before him.

"Mr. Profado…"

"Is Father Joe in?"

"He's inside," Mike answered, stoically.

"Great!"

Wally promptly headed for the front door of the rectory.

"What's up with that?" April asked, curiously.

"I don't like him," Mike replied.

"Why not?"

"From what I know, he's the one that made sure charges were brought against me. Some church brother he is!"

April wasn't sure how to respond.

"What does he have against you?" she asked, moments later.

"Beats me. As much as I see him around this place, I don't believe he and I said more than a few words to each other. So, I don't know what his problem is. Maybe Mom's right. Maybe he's trying to get back at her by trying to bury me!"

"I heard the rumors a while back. You never know with people these days." She slid on her gloves.

"No. You never know."

* * * *

"Wally, come right in!" Joe greeted him at the door. "Nice, sunny day. Isn't it?"

Wally walked inside. "Yes, Father. I hope they're wrong about rain being in the forecast." He sat on the couch.

"I surely hope they are. I was thinking of hitting the beach for an hour or two to get a swim and suntan before the day is out."

Wally chuckled. "You still like the beach, huh?"

Joe grimaced. "Why would I stop enjoying the beach? My doc told me last week my magnesium level is low. I figured besides the supplements, I'd soak some up from the sea. That's the natural stuff there." He took a seat on the sofa.

"You're right about that."

Joe crossed his legs. "I wanna thank you for coming by when you had a few minutes to spare," he said. "I didn't want to bombard you at work again and thought maybe here would be a good setting for us to have a brief chat."

"Okay."

"Just give me a moment." He got up abruptly and headed over to the front door.

"Oh! Hello, April!" He waved. "How are you doing today?"

"Hi, Father Joe. I'm fine, thanks," she answered.

"Great! Helping out with the gardening, I see."

"Yes, sir. Thought I'd be productive while I'm waiting for Mom's meeting to end."

"That's awesome!" He said. "Mike, would you please go to the other side of the yard where Mr. Pickling is working and ask him to give you a handful of those orchids. They would add some color to the new garden."

"Yes, Father," Mike replied.

"Take April with you!"

The teenagers walked off together and now that Joe had gotten rid of them for a while, he was ready to speak with Wally.

The detective was quietly twiddling his thumbs when Joe returned to the living room.

"Now that that's settled, let's get down to business," Joe told him. "I have a question for you, Wally."

"Uh-huh?"

"I'm trying to understand the rather obscure series of events that went from Mother Elizabeth's dead body being discovered to Mike Tenney's arrest."

"Okay…"

"I am no detective, but something stood out to me as it relates to Mother's issue with Mike in the days preceding her death."

Wally waited patiently.

"Weren't the police informed that she had complained to me about him after the incident?"

"Uh—yes. We knew."

"Well…why wasn't I questioned? No one came to me to find out what was discussed or anything of the sort. Why not?"

Wally thought for a moment. "I'm not sure. It must've been an oversight."

"An oversight?" Joe frowned. "Isn't it the detective's job to make sure that every lead is followed up on entirely?"

"Yes, it is—as a matter of fact."

"What about other areas of the ministry that Mother Elizabeth was involved in?"

"What about them?" Wally asked.

"Were the people she often interacted with in those various ministries contacted and interviewed to find out if anything occurred lately that might have been remotely alarming?" Joe probed.

Wally hesitated briefly. "I'm not sure about that. The nuns were all interrogated privately subsequent to the group interview that you and the archbishop attended."

"Yes, I heard about that. But you know I'm not talking about the nuns."

"I know." He sighed deeply.

"Which detective is actually working this case, Wally?" Joe was clearly concerned.

"Detective Kenna and I are working the case."

"I ask because there's some real disconnect here. The investigation appears disjointed to me."

"In what way, Father?"

"It seems to me like Mike was pinpointed from the beginning, probably due to the disagreement he and Mother Elizabeth had shortly before her death. And because of that, you guys don't appear to have looked in any other direction. I'm very uncomfortable knowing that Mother had countless interactions and not even a decent fraction of them were explored. I'm not accusing anybody, so please don't take what I'm about to say next as an accusation or suspicion on my part because it isn't."

"Okay..."

"Sister Anna Gunter discovered the body; by her account—even pulled the knife out of her chest. Yet, she doesn't appear to have ever been the focus of the matter. Whose fingerprints were on that knife?"

"Hers," Wally admitted, "But the real killer could've easily used gloves which means that Sister Anna's prints naturally would've been the only ones there."

"You were able to give Sister Anna the benefit of the doubt and not Mike? Seems like someone has it in for him for sure."

"You're not seeing the facts as we are, Father," Wally said.

"I'm not?" Joe arched his brow.

"No. You're not. We are not amateurs at this. I have fifteen years in homicide division and Detective Kenna has eleven. We know what we're doing. And if a viable lead was not explored, it only could've been an oversight, like I said."

Joe uncrossed his legs and leaned forward. "Charlie Mullings—he was an oversight too?"

"Who?"

"*Charlie Mullings*. Did you ever even listen to what the nuns were telling you? Or is it that your individual interrogations were not that detailed?"

Wally was silent.

"Mr. Mullings is a gentleman who lives just down the street from the convent. He and Mother Elizabeth had a big to-do and the man refused to ever go back to the convent to get food. Instead, a couple of the nuns used to stop by his house and give him groceries. What about the passerby Peter Callaghan who told me he happened to see a strange man on the convent grounds the night before Mother Elizabeth's body was discovered? I showed him Mike's picture and he did not identify him as being the man he saw. He was adamant about it. You know what else he was adamant about?"

"What?"

"Not talking to the police because you all never bothered to question residents in the surrounding area."

"Is that what he said?"

"Precisely. This guy might hold the clue to solving Mother Elizabeth's murder case—and helping to bring the real killer to justice."

"Where can we find this man?" Wally asked.

Joe retrieved his wallet and handed him a yellow piece of paper with names and directions on it.

"Has time of death been established?" Joe asked.

"Yes. Mother Elizabeth died at approximately 11:50 P.M., the night before her body was discovered," Wally replied.

"Do your job, Wally. And this time, don't leave any stones unturned. A young man's life and freedom depend on it."

$\mathcal{J}$oe was not about to leave Mike's life and freedom in Wally Profado's hand, but he certainly wanted him to finally get busy conducting a proper investigation of the case.

Jim Cruz had provided Henry Sears' address an hour earlier and Joe had deliberately failed to mention his name to Wally so that he could get to him first.

After Wally left, he hopped into his car and took the highway for Cedarsborough—the subdivision where Henry allegedly resided.

Cedarsborough was a large subdivision on the western end of Old Providence. It was rumored in the McCullen family that Joe's second cousin Thomas once purchased a house in that area before he and his wife Rosa abruptly sold it and moved away for good. They'd only lived there for seven months. Thomas had sworn that the place was swarming with ghosts, but no one paid him any mind. And they surely didn't get that many visitors either.

The drive to Cedarsborough took approximately twenty-five minutes. Joe pulled up in front of a green single storey house that looked like it was begging for attention. He got out of the car, walked up to the porch and rang the doorbell. Within seconds, the door swung open.

"Yeah?" Henry Sears appeared right in front of him. In real life, he mirrored the way he looked on his social media profile.

"Henry Sears?" Joe asked, knowingly.

"Uh-huh. What can I do you for?"

"My name is Father Joe McCullen. I was wondering if I can have a few minutes of your time. May I come in?"

Henry thought for a moment. "It depends on for what."

"I'd like to speak with you about your sister, Maggie."

"What about her?" he asked.

Joe glanced around. "I really think we should talk inside, if you don't mind."

Henry invited him in.

The interior of the house had been forsaken like the rest of the property. Magazines

174

and clothes were strewn across the chairs and used beer cans sat on the center table.

"Have a seat wherever you can find the room, Father," Henry told him.

"Thank you," Joe replied. He moved a red jacket over and sat on the sofa.

Henry sat across from him.

"You might as well come clean, Henry," Joe said. "I know what you did."

"Did? Did like what?" Henry grimaced. "I have no idea what you're talking about."

"I know about your sister, and I want to express how very sorry I am for your loss."

Henry was now silent, but Joe instantly noticed the shift in his demeanor. He seemed somewhat anxious.

"When a loved one takes their own life, oftentimes, it's a different level of pain that the family are left to cope with," Joe continued.

"You need to drop it!" Henry got up and walked over to a nearby window.

"Henry…I need you to hear me out. I know you loved your sister dearly and what happened to her was very unfortunate…"

Henry turned and glared at him. "It was wrong, Father! Say it! It was wrong!"

Joe was looking at a man riddled with pain and he felt deeply for him.

"Say it!" Henry insisted.

"I believe the situation could've been handled better—with more care and compassion," Joe said.

"You refuse to say it, don't you? You refuse to say that what that mother superior or whatever she's called did to Maggie was plain wrong."

"I know that this is a delicate subject, but by all accounts, it seemed that the consecrated life was perhaps not Maggie's calling."

"That's where you're wrong." He pointed at Joe, finding his seat again. "Being a nun was what Maggie dreamed of ever since she was a little girl. Our parents took us to church nearly every time the doors were opened and Maggie fell in love with it—not only with the church, but with God. She saw nuns doing things to help make other people's lives better and she admired and wanted to emulate them. And finally, to be given the chance to fulfill her calling, and then for that witch to kick her out shortly afterwards, was devastating. When she came back home, all she did was cry. She even went to find that woman months later to try and convince her to take her back, and she refused. There was nothing I could do to console my sister. Lord knows I tried everything and, in the end, after she couldn't take it anymore, she…"

It's a real tragedy," Joe said, glancing at Maggie's photograph on the wall. She had a round, pleasant face, blonde hair just like her brother and a mole near her nose. Joe gathered that Maggie was indeed the woman Adele Smith had claimed visited Mother Elizabeth the night of the Beginners meeting. He'd found out from the archbishop just hours earlier that within days of confronting Mother Elizabeth that final time at the church, the woman hanged herself.

"That's why that nun had to die," Henry continued. He looked at Joe intently. "Can I make a confession right here and now, Father?"

"Yes, you can."

"Let me make it clear that I'm not seeking absolution because I'm not sorry for my sins—at least not this one, anyway. But I do know that confession is good for the soul and who better to confess to than a priest who must keep all my dirty, little secrets?" He had a smirk on his face.

Joe wasn't about to stop him. He'd gone there for the truth and didn't intend to leave without it.

They both made the sign of the cross.

"Bless me, Father, for I have sinned. It's been two years and six months since my last confession…"

"I encourage you to be entirely truthful, Henry, as you and I both know it is the only way to live and to have peace of mind," Joe said.

Henry was sitting upright, his back resting comfortably against the chair. "There's no way I wasn't gonna avenge my sister's death, Father. I'm just glad my parents weren't alive to experience the loss of their only daughter."

"How'd you get in?" Joe asked him.

For a moment, Henry was still engrossed in his own thoughts. "What? Get in where?"

"The convent. The night you killed Mother Elizabeth."

"Oh. That part was easy-peasy." He smiled. "Our cousin Claire Hans just opened the side door and let me in after everyone had gone off to bed. I waited in the dark and when the old hag got up, I guess to go to the bathroom or something, that's when I struck. That knife of mine got her good."

Joe was repulsed by his account.

"And afterwards?"

Claire let me out so she could lock the door behind me. It's as simple as that."

"As awful as the deed you committed was, I'm now wondering why you chose to kill her there at the convent."

"Why not? It was her home. *Home*, where I live—in that garage…" he pointed, "was where my sister died. I figured it was only fitting that the woman who was responsible for her death would meet her own fate in her place of residence. Understand me?"

He had an angry glare in his eyes.

"You do know you were wrong. Don't you, Henry?" Joe said. "From what you told me about your childhood, you were raised better than that. What about: *Thou shalt not kill?*"

"The Old Testament says: *An eye for an eye and a tooth for a tooth*," Henry countered.

"Henry, I will not sit here and act like Mother Elizabeth Rhinehart was perfect. None of us are. We all have our flaws, but she dismissed your sister for a legitimate reason that day.

179

Maggie was caught outside being intimate with a young man. For goodness' sake, she was at a convent and there to be a nun! Obviously, she was not sure of her calling, Henry. In this instance, Mother Elizabeth made what she felt was the right call to send your sister home to rethink her vocation."

"It *was* her vocation!" he yelled. "She made one dumb mistake and was kicked out forever because of it? That wasn't right. What happened to second chances and forgiveness, and all that religious stuff you priests teach? Maggie made one mistake! Just one! And it shouldn't have caused her her life."

Joe leaned forward. "Henry…listen to me. You've got to go to the police and tell the truth. Just come clean about what happened and the court may show you mercy. God certainly will."

"Not doing it, Father."

"A young man's life is on the line here. Mike Tenney has been accused of the crime you committed. You must make things right."

"It's a pity… I agree. But I have nothing to say about it," he replied. "It's a dog-eat-dog world. And you'd just be wasting your time telling the cops about my so-called confession—even if you went against your oath. It'll just be hearsay and that's inadmissible in court."

"The phone call. Who made it?" Joe asked.

"What phone call?"

"The one someone made to the police claiming they heard Mike threaten Mother Elizabeth's life the week before the murder," Joe explained.

"Oh! That was Claire! It was all a part of the plan. You don't know what I had to go through to convince her to do it. She's so scary and all."

Joe was amazed by the whole story and how Claire had been roped into such a crime after having lived a remarkable life.

Just then, the front door of the house swung open and a giant of a man wearing blue jeans, a white T-shirt, dark shades and a cowboy hat rushed in with a handgun.

Joe and Henry immediately stood up.

Jim Cruz walked in behind him, along with another man who also carried a handgun.

"We've got all we need on camera," Jim said, nonchalantly as his PI, Donald Angler, slapped handcuffs on Henry.

Henry was visibly shocked.

"You set me up, priest!" he snarled.

"You've got it all wrong, bud," Jim coolly interjected. "Father Joe had no idea we followed him here and we came prepared, just in case. Set up shop right outside that window over there and caught your entire confession on camera. I'm glad to know you ratted out your cousin too. She'll be in handcuffs next."

Henry was escorted outside to a waiting truck.

"What made you follow me here?" Joe asked Jim, still startled by their unexpected intrusion.

"Don recognized this guy's name when I asked him to check out the address for you. Henry Sears was arrested a year ago for assaulting his girlfriend; spent three months in the can. And I figured if you'd asked about this guy, you must've suspected he was involved somehow in Mother Elizabeth's murder or at least knew something. So, I decided to tail you since you weren't forthcoming about it earlier," Jim explained.

They walked outside together.

"What's gonna happen now?"

"Don has the right to make citizen arrests, so he's gonna transport the guy to the police station where he'll show them the evidence. I'm sure they'll be picking up his relative at the convent right afterwards."

Joe watched as Henry was driven away from the scene, seated in the backseat of the truck. He was sitting next to the other armed man who'd entered the house.

"You did well, Father Joe, but I told you to leave the detective work to us. If we didn't show up, there's no telling what this guy would've done to you after he went and spilled his guts."

Joe sighed. "It's such a tragedy, Jim. The whole thing is such a tragedy. Two people lost their lives and two are about to lose their freedom."

"At least with the evidence we now have in our possession, Mike will be vindicated," Jim said.

"You're right! God is good and prayer changes things. Thank you, brother."

He gave Jim a pat on the back.

14

"How dare you?" Gertrude glared at Claire Hans as she was being handcuffed. All the other nuns had gathered together in the hallway behind the police. Wally Profado was with the arresting officer.

Nervous and sweating, Claire lowered her head.

"Wait right there, officer. I've got something to say to this woman!" Gertrude insisted. The officer didn't think twice to obey.

She got within two feet of her fellow sister. "You came into this convent, made your vows to God, befriended all of us and in the end, conspired to have our Mother Superior killed. You are a shame and disgrace to yourself as a woman and to this sacred institution. Mother Elizabeth was a difficult woman, but she didn't deserve to die, especially after she stood for what was right in this instance. I will pray for your soul Sister Claire and for everything you hold dear. You will have a lot of time to think about what you've done."

Claire did not utter a single word in response and was thereafter escorted out of the convent. Many of the nuns stood watching in tears with the realization that the woman they'd come to know and love had betrayed them all.

Angelica went over to be with Gertrude who was visibly upset.

"Why did she do it?" Gertrude asked.

"Her cousin Maggie," Angelica said. "Maybe they used to be close. And maybe she hated Mother Elizabeth more than she ever cared to admit."

15

The following morning…

Sue hugged her son tightly after Jim had notified Joe by phone that all of the charges against Mike had been dropped.

"I can't tell you how elated I am!" She had tears of joy in her eyes.

"Me too," Mike said, smiling from ear to ear.

They were standing in the living room inside of the rectory.

"We all are glad that you've been vindicated, Mike," Joe added.

"If it wasn't for you, it wouldn't have happened," Mike said. And Sue was nodding in agreement.

"That's where you're wrong," Joe told him. "I was just a vessel God used. If it wasn't me, it would've been someone else. Either way, you would've been all right."

Mike went and gave him a bear hug. Joe ruffled the top of his hair.

"You're the best, Father Joe! You're like the dad I never had. Did I ever tell you that?"

"I don't think so."

Joe proceeded to sit down and Sue did the same.

"Well, you are—and I just want you to know that I really appreciate you."

"Now that this whole thing is over, let your mother here be able to appreciate those grades of yours. And keep out of fist fights if you know what's good for you," Joe answered. "It doesn't matter what anyone says to you. It takes a real man to walk away from nonsense. Ya hear?"

"I hear you, Father," he replied.

"I hope so—because as you now see, trouble is easy to get into and hard to get out of. Hotheadedness and failing to control your anger are what they conveniently used against you as circumstantial evidence to build a case. It was easy for them."

"I see what you mean," Mike said.

Just then, there was a knock at the door and Mike went to open it.

On the other side was Wally Profado.

"Mike…" he said, rather quietly.

"Wally, come on in!" Joe spotted him from the living room.

Mike was hesitant to step aside as he and Wally locked eyes.

"Your legs can't move, all of a sudden, Mike?" Joe asked the boy.

He soon stepped aside and Wally walked in.

"Good morning, everyone," he said.

Sue didn't bother to respond.

"I thought I'd come by to say how glad I am that Mike here is no longer on the hook for Mother Elizabeth's death."

"He's right behind you." Joe gestured to the detective.

"Sorry," he said, turning to Mike and feeling a little embarrassed. "Mike, I'm sorry about what you went through. Believe me, this wasn't any kind of personal vendetta against you or your mother. I was…we all were just doing our jobs."

"Quite inefficiently," Sue remarked.

"Maybe so. As a matter of fact, I can't run from that. We obviously jumped to conclusions and did so prematurely. I hope you'd accept my apology, son."

The young man stood there looking at the man—a fellow parishioner—he had almost come to hate. In that moment, all he could think about was how he'd nearly ruined his life and in spite of that, what Joe would expect for him to do. Moreover, what God required him to do.

He soon extended his hand. "I'm not your *son*, but I accept your apology."

They both shook hands and Joe was smiling proudly.

Sue, though proud of her son's maturity and capacity to forgive, was still annoyed and disgusted by Wally Profado.

"That's all I came by to say," Wally said.

"Thank you, Wally," Joe told him. "It takes a big man to admit his faults."

"Yep. Anyway...I'd better get back to work."

"Let me walk you to the door." Joe got up.

Before he left, Wally turned to him and said, "You know, Mike is lucky to have you as a spiritual Father. We all are."

"You're too kind."

Joe then thought of something. "Tell me, Wally. To your knowledge, was it Sister Claire who made the call about Mike having threatened Mother Elizabeth?"

"The call came in anonymously to Detective Kenna. The caller refused to give her name, but Kenna remembered Claire's voice and so, we all suspected it was her. Kenna subsequently spoke with Claire, but she insisted that she hadn't made the call. And I wasn't at liberty to share that information with you or anyone outside the investigation at that time," Wally explained.

Joe nodded. "Thanks again for coming, Wally. Be safe out there."

"Thanks, Father."

Joe was amazed at the nerve of the detectives to try and build a case entirely on hearsay and circumstantial evidence. And thought it was ludicrous that they arrested and charged Mike based on an anonymous tip—the allegations of which would likely never have been substantiated.

After Wally left, Joe looked at Sue. "I know that telling you to let it go is easier said than done, Sue, but do your son and yourself a favor and let it go. None of us can change what's already been done and certainly none of us needs to remain in the past. We've only got here, now—today. Let's live in the moment, appreciating all that we have and all the blessings we have been given. Can you do that?"

Glancing at her son, she readily replied. "Yes. I can do it."

* * * *

Joe acknowledged all of the guards as he steadily made his way down Block C of the local prison. He'd walked that route and those grounds many times before, but this time was special. Block C was where Sister Claire Hans had made her new home.

She was sitting quietly at the cold, steel desk awaiting his arrival and she wondered what he would say to her and what her response would be; whether she'd hold back or freely admit the truth. She was no longer one of them—one of the sisters, one who dedicated herself and her soul to the consecrated life. She was now just Claire— that woman who was nothing special to anyone. At least, that's what she thought. The same woman who, as a kid, got overlooked almost every time while the more bubbly, extroverted kids got all the attention. It was the same way in the house she grew up in. Quiet, shy Claire was nearly invisible to her parents while her siblings constantly got their way.

The male guard was standing just outside the door when Joe finally arrived.

"Good evening!" Joe said to him in the same cheerful manner he'd used with the others. However, inside he felt almost sick to his stomach knowing that he was about to visit a nun who had knowingly participated in a most despicable crime.

"Good evening, Father," the guard replied, just before opening the door to the little white room where Claire was being held.

Joe noticed the look of shame on her face as she sat there quietly. As the guard shut the door behind him, he pulled out the metal chair and sat down.

For a few moments and with a heavy heart, he only looked at her, but she avoided making eye contact.

"Sister Claire…" he finally said.

"Yes, Father." She glanced at him, then immediately lowered her head.

"Look at me."

Claire seemed to struggle with it, but eventually made eye contact.

"How are you doing?"

"I'm here, so I guess you can probably imagine," she replied, quietly.

"Do you need anything?" he asked.

She slowly shook her head. "No."

Seeing her there in a red prison suit and wearing ankle chains felt surreal to him. But even so, he could not deny the reality of the moment.

"Why did you do it, Sister?" He yearned for an answer that made sense, but in his heart he knew it was impossible.

She looked away for a few moments, then said, "I knew that you were going to ask that question and in a way, I dreaded it."

"Why?"

She shifted a bit in her chair. "Because the truth sometimes, Father, can be uglier and darker than you ever imagined it could be, especially when you've hidden it from those you love for so long."

"Who are you referring to?"

"My sisters in the convent—especially Angelica, who was always so nice to me. Yet, as nice and kind as she is, I knew I couldn't possibly utter words to her that were deep inside my heart. The simple truth is that I'm a coward. If I had made it a practice to speak up more like some of the others did, Mother Elizabeth might be alive today. I couldn't speak up to Mother when she said awful things that hurt my feelings and I couldn't even speak up for Maggie after she was dismissed. Maybe if I did, Mother would've given her a second chance and both of them would be here today. Instead, I kept my mouth shut and quietly grieved for Maggie as she struggled to cope afterwards."

"How is it that no one at the convent knew that you and Maggie were related?" Joe asked.

"It was Mother Elizabeth's idea to keep it confidential. She already wasn't keen about the idea of family members living there together. But Maggie and I are distant cousins; that's the only reason she allowed it," Claire explained.

It was obvious to Joe that their mother superior was very good at keeping secrets when she wanted to.

"How did Henry convince you to let him in that night, Sister?"

She cleared her throat. "He told me that Maggie committed suicide shortly after she went and pleaded with Mother for a second chance and she denied her. That's when he told me his plan and that he needed my help. I felt so awful for Maggie, and even so, I refused to help him."

And…?" Joe was patiently waiting.

"He called me a coward and said that I was betraying the family. I already felt partially responsible for what happened to Maggie because I didn't approach Mother on her behalf before she was driven to suicide. So, it was no longer a difficult decision for me to make. And I guess another thing is…" She paused for a moment. "Deep inside, I loathed Mother."

Joe was surprised that she actually said the words.

"I just didn't have the guts to admit it like Sister Rosa did. Mother made my life miserable for so many years and I just accepted everything she said and did in order to keep the peace. The ugliness I mentioned was when my repeated attempts to keep the peace morphed into hatred and resentment like I'd never felt before for another human being. I prayed about this so many times, but couldn't seem to think any differently about her. When Maggie died and I saw the pain in her brother's eyes, I guess the hidden hatred had taken over and I'm afraid, the rest is history."

Joe was trying to digest everything that Claire had said.

"Can you do me a favor, Father?" she asked.

"Sure. What is it?" he replied.

"Can you please tell Mike Tenney that I'm very sorry and it was nothing personal? I used the falling out Mother had with him to ensure that attention from the police was diverted away from any of us at the convent. It was Henry's idea for me to place an anonymous call to the police reporting a supposed threat that Mike made against Mother Elizabeth. Of course, it was a lie and I didn't wanna do it, but there Henry went with that name-calling again and putting a guilt trip on me. I know it's not an excuse."

The Claire Hans sitting in front of him that day seemed like a completely different person—a stranger. Perhaps, in many ways she was—even to herself.

"Can I pray for you, Sister?" Joe asked, tenderly.

She readily accepted his kind offer.

~ THE END ~

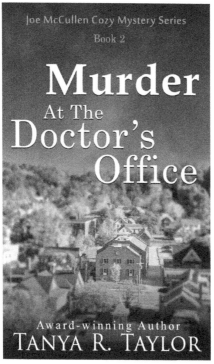

Dr. Mark Bridges had no idea that the couple walking into his office that day would change his life and his practice forever.

Melanie Robinson needed the help of a good doctor and she was convinced she'd found him. After all, Dr. Bridges was entering his twentieth year of practice and knew what he was doing. Or did he?

Had his years of treating patients made him less sympathetic to their needs or what happened in Melanie's case was simply her fate?

And who would he have to answer to?

Don't miss this intriguing episode in the Joe McCullen Cozy Mystery Series.

A COZY MYSTERY SERIES THAT WILL
HAVE YOU LAUGHING YOUR PANTS OFF!

Lucille Pfiffer sees, but not with her eyes. She lives with her beloved dog Vanilla ("Nilla" for short) in a cozy neighborhood that is quite "active" due to what occurred in the distant past.

Though totally blind, she plays an integral role in helping to solve pressing and puzzling mysteries, one right after the other, which, without her, might remain unsolved.

The question is: How can she do any of that with such a handicap?

#1 Bestseller and #1 New Release!

BLIND SIGHT

Book 1 – Lucille Pfiffer Mystery Series

1

Super Vanilla

I carefully descended the air-conditioned jitney and started down the sidewalk with my cane in hand and Nilla, my pet Shih Tzu on leash at my side. Taking a cab was our preferred mode of transport, but sometimes we enjoyed a nice, long bus ride instead. Nestled on both sides of the street were a number of shops, including convenience stores, jewelry, liquor, antique stores and haberdashery.

It was the day before my scheduled meeting with the local pet society that while walking along downtown Chadsworth, I heard a woman scream. The vision of her anguished face flashed into my mind and the image of a young boy dressed in faded blue jeans and a long-sleeved black shirt running at full speed in the direction Nilla and I were headed. Gripped tightly in his hand was a purse that did not belong to him; his eyes bore a mixture of confidence in his escape intertwined with fear of capture. He was quickly approaching—now only several feet behind us. In no time, he would turn the bend just ahead and be long gone bearing the ill-gotten fruits of his labor.

One could imagine how many times he'd done the same thing and gotten away with it, only to plan his next move – to stealthily lie in wait for his unsuspecting victim. I heard the squish-squashing of his tennis shoes closely behind. It was the precise moment he was about to zoom past us that I abruptly held out my cane to the left, tripping him, and watched as he fell forward, rolling over like a car tire, then ultimately landing flat on his back on the hard pavement. I dropped the leash and yelled, "Get him, Nilla!"

Nilla took off at full speed and pounced on top of the already injured boy, biting him on every spot she could manage – determined to teach him a lesson he'd never forget. He screamed and tried to push her off of him, but a man dashed over and pinned him to the ground. I made my way over to Nilla and managed to get her away from the chaotic scene. Her job was done. As tiny as she was, she made her Momma proud.

The frantic woman got her purse back and the boy was restrained until police arrived.

2

_____

The room was almost packed to capacity when I arrived at the podium with the gracious assistance of a young man. As he went to take his seat in the front row, I proceeded with my introduction: "My name's Lucille Pfiffer—Mrs., that is—even though my husband Donnie has been dead and gone for the past four and a half years now. We had no children, other than our little Shih Tzu, Vanilla; 'Nilla' for short." I smiled, reflectively. "By the way, I must tell you she doesn't respond to 'Nill' or 'Nillie'; it's 'Nilla' if you stand a chance of getting her attention. She totally ignores you sometimes even when you call her by her legal name '*Va (vuh)*…nilla'.

"We reside in a quiet part of town known as Harriet's Cove. A little neighborhood with homes and properties of all sizes. We're mostly middle class folk, pretending to be upper class. The ones with large homes, much bigger than my split level, are the ones you hardly see strolling around the neighborhood, and they certainly don't let their kids play with yours if you've got any. Those kids are the 'sheltered' ones—they stay indoors mainly, other than when it's time to hop in the family car and go wherever for whatever."

I heard the rattle inside someone's throat.

"Uh, Mrs. Pfiffer…" A gentleman at the back of the room stood up. "I don't mean to be rude or anything, but you mentioned the neighbors' kids as if you can see these things you described going on in your neighborhood. I mean, how you said some don't play with others and they only come out when they're about to leave the house. But how do you know any of this? Or should we assume, it's by hearsay?"

I admired his audacity to interrupt an old lady while she's offering a requested and well-meaning introduction to herself. After all, I was a newbie to the Pichton Pet Society and their reputation for having some 'snobby' members preceded them.

"Thank you very much, sir, for the questions you raised," I answered. "Yes, you are to assume that I know some of this—just some—

via hearsay. The rest I know from living in my neck of the woods for the past thirty-five years. I haven't always been blind, you know." I liked how they put you front and center on the little platform to give your introductory speech. That way, no eyes could miss you and you think, for one delusionary moment, that you're the cream of the crop. Made a woman my age feel really special. After all, at sixty-eight, three months and four days, and a little *over-the-hill*, I highly doubted there were going to be any young studs falling head over heels in love with me and showering me with their attention.

"Pardon me, ma'am." He gave a brief nod and sat back down again.

I took that as an apology. I could see the look on Merlene's face as she sat in the fourth row from the front. She thought I'd blown my cover for a minute there, but she keeps forgetting that I'm no amateur at protecting my interests. Sure, I sometimes talk a bit too much and gotta put my foot in my mouth afterwards, but my decades of existence give me an excuse.

I could hear Merlene scolding me now:

"Lucille, I've told you time and time again, you must be careful of what you say! No

one's gonna understand how an actual blind woman can see the way you do. They won't believe you even if you told them!"

Her words were like a scorched record playing in my brain. She got on my nerves with all her warnings, but I was surely glad I was able to drag her down there to the meeting with me that day.

I tried not to face that guy's direction anymore, even though the dark sunglasses I wore served its purpose of concealing my *blind stare.* "Thank you, sir," I said. "Well, I guess there's not much left to say about me, except that I used to have a career as a private banker for about twenty years. After that, I retired to spend more time with Donnie, who'd just retired from the Military a year earlier. We spent the next twenty-one years together until he passed away from heart trouble."

Someone else stood up—this time a lady around my age. "If you don't mind my asking…at what point did you lose your eyesight? And how are you possibly able to care for your pet Vanilla?"

When I revisit that part of my life, I tend to get a tad emotional. "It was a little over eight years ago that I developed a rare disease known as Simbalio Flonilia. I know, it sounds like a deadly virus or something, but it's a progressive and rather aggressive deterioration of the retina. They don't know what causes it, but within a year of my diagnosis, I was totally blind. I'm thankful for Donnie because after it happened, he kept me sane. Needless to say, I wasn't handling being blind so well after having been able to see all of my life. Donnie was truly a lifesaver and so was Nilla. She's so smart—she gets me everything I need and she's very protective, despite her little size. I've cared for Nilla ever since she was two months old and I pretty much know where everything is regarding her. Taking care of her is the easy part. Her taking care of me is another story."

Though somewhat hazy, I could see the smiles on many of their faces. The talk of Nilla obviously softened some of their rugged features.

Mrs. Claire Fairweather, the chairperson, came and stood right next to me.

"Lucille, we are happy to welcome you as the newest member of our organization!" She spoke, eagerly. "You have obviously been a

210

productive member of Chadsworth for many years and more importantly, you are a loving mom to your precious little dog, Vanilla. People, let's give her a warm round of applause!"

A gentleman came and helped me to my chair. The fragrance he was wearing reminded me of how much Donnie loved his cologne. Such a fine man, he was. If it were up to him, I wouldn't have worked a day of my married life. It would've been enough for him to see me every day at home just looking pretty and smiling. His engineering job paid well enough, but I loved my career and since it wasn't a stressful one, I didn't feel the need to quit to just sit home and do nothing.

"Thank you, dear," I told the nice, young man.

"My pleasure, Mrs. Pfiffer."

Merlene leaned in as Claire proceeded with the meeting. "I told you—you talk too blasted much!" She whispered. "If you keep up this nonsense, they're gonna take your prized disability checks away from you."

"It'll happen over my dead body, Merlene," I calmly replied.

"Mrs. Pfiffer, I must say it's truly an honor that you've decided to join us here at the Pichton Pet Society," Claire said at the podium. "With your experience as a professional, I'm sure you'll have lots of ideas on how we can raise funds for the continued care of senior pets, stray dogs and abused animals. Your contribution to this group would be greatly appreciated."

After the meeting, she'd caught Merlene and me at the door, as we were about to head for Merlene's Toyota.

"I'm so glad you joined us, Mrs. Pfiffer. My secretary will be in touch with you about our next meeting."

"Thank you, Mrs. Fairweather. I'm honored that you accepted me. After all, animals are most precious. Anything that supports their best interest, I'm fired up for."

"Did you always love animals?" she asked.

I gulped. "Well, if I may be straight with you... I hated them— especially dogs!"

Her hand flew to her chest and a scowl crept over her face. I must have startled her by the revelation.

"It was after Nilla came into our life that I soon found a deep love and appreciation for animals—especially dogs. To me, they're just like precious little children who depend on us adults to take care of them and to show them love, as I quickly learned that they have the biggest heart for their owners."

Fairweather seemed relieved and a wide smile stretched across her face. "Oh, that's so good to know! I was afraid there for a moment that we'd made a terrible mistake by accepting you into our organization!" She laughed it off.

I did a pretend laugh back at her. I may be blind, but I'm not stupid—that woman actually just insulted me to my face!

"I don't know why you want to be a part of that crummy group with those snooty, snobbish, high society creeps anyway!" Merlene remarked after we both got in the car.

I rested my cane beside me. "Because I've been a part of crummy groups for most of my adult life. I don't know anything different."

Merlene gave me a reprimanding look. "It's not funny, Lucille. You dragged me out here to sit with people who, I admit love animals, but they seem to hate humans! I've heard some things about that Fairweather woman that'll make your eyes roll. You know she's a professor at the state college, right?"

"Uh huh."

"Well, I heard she treats the kids who register for her class really badly. She fails most of them every single term. The only ones who pass are the ones who kiss up to her."

"If there's a high failure rate in her class, why would the state keep her on then?" I asked.

"Politics. She got there through politics and is pretty much untouchable. I heard she also was a tyrant to her step-kids. Pretty much ran them all out of the house and practically drove the second fool who married her insane. He actually ended up in the loony bin and when he died, she took everything—not giving his kids a drink of water they can say they'd inherited."

"I blame the husband for that."

"Not when she got him to sign over everything to her in his will when he wasn't in his right mind. The whole thing was contested, but because she was politically connected, she came out on top. After that, she moved on to husband number three. If I knew that woman was the chairperson of this meeting you dragged me out to, I would've waited in the car for you instead of sitting in the same room with her."

We were almost home when Merlene finally stopped talking about Fairweather. You'd think the woman didn't have a life of her own, considering the length of time she focused on this one individual she obviously couldn't stand. I just wanted to get the hell out of that hot car (the two front windows of which couldn't roll down), and get home to my Nilla. She'd be waiting near the door for me for sure.

I wish I was allowed to bring her to the meeting. They claimed they're all about animals, but not one was in that room. I guess I was being unfair since they mentioned that particular Monday meeting was the only one they couldn't bring their pets to. That was the meeting where new members were introduced and important plans for fundraisers were often discussed.

"I'll see you later, Lucille. Going home to do some laundry," Merlene said after pulling up onto my driveway. "Need help getting out?"

"I'm good," I replied.

"How sharp is it now?"

"I can see the outline of your face. Nothing else at the moment. Everything was almost crystal clear in the meeting."

"Yeah. Inopportune time for it to have been crystal clear," Merlene mumbled.

She was used to my *inner vision*, as we call it, going in and out like that. I grabbed hold of my cane and the tip of it hit the ground as I turned to get out of the vehicle. "I can manage just fine. I'm sure it'll come back when it feels like. Thanks for coming out with me."

I smiled as I thought of how much she often sacrificed for me. Ten years my junior, Merlene was a good friend. We had a row almost every day, but we loved one another. She and I were like the typical married couple.

"By the way, I forgot to mention, my tenant Theodore, told me this morning that someone had called about renting the last vacant room."

"Perfect!" Merlene said.

"Said he was coming by this afternoon. What time is it?"

"It's a quarter of five."

I had an idea. "Merlene, he's supposed to show up at five o'clock. You wanna hang around for a few minutes to see what my prospects are? Maybe he's tall, dark and handsome and I may stand a chance."

"I doubt it," she squawked. "Besides, I must get at least a load of laundry done today. If not, I'll likely have to double up tomorrow for as quick as that boy goes through clothes! I tell ya, ever since he met that Delilah, he's changed so much."

"Why don't you leave that boy alone?" I barked. "He's twenty-seven-years-old, for Heaven's sake! Allow him to date whomever the hell he feels like. He's gotta live and learn, you know, and buck his head when need be. You and I went through it and so must he. You surely didn't allow your folks to tell you who you ought to date and who you shouldn't, did you? And furthermore, why do you keep calling Juliet, *Delilah*?"

"Because she's just like that Delilah woman in the Bible; can't be trusted!" Merlene spoke her mind. "And since you asked—why do you call her *Juliet*? Her name's Sabrina."

I sighed. "You know why I call her that."

"I tell ya...she's no Juliet!"

"Anyway, you're gonna wait with me a few minutes while I interview this newcomer or not?" I'd just had enough of Merlene's bickering for one day.

I heard her roll up the two remaining car windows and pull her key out of the ignition. It was one among a ring of keys.

Nilla was right at the front door when I let myself in. I leaned down and scooped up my little princess. She licked my face and I could feel the soft vibration of her wagging tail. Merlene walked in behind me.

"Nilla pilla!" she said, as she plonked down on the sofa. "Why can't you assist Mommy here with her interview? After all, you've gotta live with the newbie too."

I heard Theodore's footsteps descending the staircase. His was a totally different vibration from Anthony's. Anthony's steps were softer like that of a woman's feet. I had a good look at him a few times and he definitely was *Mister*

Debonair. And that desk job he had at the computer company suited him just fine. Theodore was different; he was more hardcore, a blue collar worker at the welding plant, pee sprinkling the toilet seat kinda guy. That was my biggest problem with him – he wasn't all that tidy, especially in the bathroom. But I hadn't kicked him out already because he's got good manners and sort of treats me like I'm his mother. Anthony mostly stays to himself and that's fine with me too.

After I'd sat down, Nilla wiggled constantly to get out of my arms. She didn't like "hands" as much as she preferred dashing all over the place, particularly when her energy level was high. I could tell that was the case at the moment, so I gently let her down on the tiled floor and immediately saw her sprinting through the wide hallway which led into the kitchen, then doubling back into the living room seconds later, and making her way under the sofa. Under there was her favorite spot in the entire house. Often, she stayed in her hut-like habitat for hours at a time.

"Good evening, ladies," Theodore said as he entered the living room. How did the meeting go?"

"It was horrible!" Merlene replied.

"It went fine, Theodore. Beautiful atmosphere; beautiful people," I said.

"She got her fifteen minutes of fame," Merlene snapped. "That's all she cares about. She should've invited *you* to waste a full two hours there instead of me."

Theodore laughed. "Well, I'll be heading out to work. See you later."

"Yeah, later," Merlene replied.

As Theodore opened the door, he met someone standing on the other side. "Oh, I'm sorry. Almost bumped into you," he said.

Theodore went his way and the person stepped inside.

"What're you doing here, David?" Merlene asked.

"I'm here to see Miss Lucille. I'm interested in renting the room."

I could sense Merlene's shock. After all, why would her son who lives with her come to rent a room from me?

Alan Danzabar has been accused of participating in a blatant bank robbery that resulted in the shooting death of a security guard.

All fingers are pointing at Alan by others who have been arrested and ultimately confessed to the crime, but Alan insists that he is innocent.

Will he get off the hook with the help of J. Wilfred & Company, particularly an employee there by the name of Barbara Sandosa who takes it upon herself to dig much deeper to uncover the truth in ways that her boss would never dream of? Or will Alan Danzabar be exposed as a liar and a killer?

Series overview:

Barbara Sandosa, a pastry lover and avid cook, works in her small town's most reputable law firm.

And although she's been hired to do a particular job, she finds herself prying into the private lives of her boss's clients, unbeknownst to them and drags young Harry Buford along for the "rocky" ride. What she uncovers in some cases shocks the innocent minds of those in her community, including her level-headed boss who's being handsomely paid to defend all who have retained his services.

Will Barbara's curiosity literally save the day or will it get her into deep trouble - possibly costing her her job?

FICTION TITLES BY TANYA R. TAYLOR

Visit Tanya's website: Tanya-R-Taylor.com

* LUCILLE PFIFFER MYSTERY SERIES
Blind Sight
Blind Escape
Blind Justice
Blind Fury
Blind Flames
Blind Risk
Blind Vacation

* INFESTATION: A Small Town Nightmare
(The Complete Series)

* THE REAL ILLUSIONS SERIES
Real Illusions: The Awakening
Real Illusions II: REBIRTH
Real Illusions III: BONE OF MY BONE
Real Illusions IV: WAR ZONE

* CORNELIUS SAGA SERIES
Cornelius (Book 1 in the Cornelius saga. *Each book in this series can stand-alone.*)

Cornelius' Revenge (Book 2 in the Cornelius saga)

CARA: Some Children Keep Terrible Secrets (Book 3 in the Cornelius saga)

We See No Evil (Book 4 in the Cornelius saga)

The Contract: Murder in The Bahamas (Book 5 in the Cornelius saga)

The Lost Children of Atlantis (Book 6 in the Cornelius saga)

Death of an Angel (Book 7 in the Cornelius saga)

The Groundskeeper (Book 8 in the Cornelius saga)

Cara: The Beginning - Matilda's Story (Book 9 in the Cornelius saga)

The Disappearing House (Book 10 in the Cornelius saga)

Wicked Little Saints (Book 11 in the Cornelius saga)

A Faint Whisper (Book 12 in the Cornelius saga)

'Til Death Do Us Part (Book 13 in the Cornelius saga)

* THE NICK MYERS SERIES
Hidden Sins Revealed (A Crime Thriller - Nick Myers Series Book 1)

Made in the USA
Las Vegas, NV
07 December 2022

61447714R00125